D1457518

SEAL TOGETHER

SILVER SEALS SERIES

MARYANN JORDAN

SEAL Together (Silver SEAL Series) Copyright 2019

All rights reserved. No part of this book may be reproduced or transmitted in any form or by any means, electronic or mechanical, including photocopying, recording, or by any information storage and retrieval system without the written permission of the author, except where permitted by law.

If you are reading this book and did not purchase it, then you are reading an illegal pirated copy. If you would be concerned about working for no pay, then please respect the author's work! Make sure that you are only reading a copy that has been officially released by the author.

This book is a work of fiction. Names, characters, places, and incidents either are products of the author's imagination or are used fictitiously. Any resemblance to actual persons, living or dead, events, or locales is entirely coincidental.

Cover Design by: Becky McGraw

Editor: Shannon Brandee Eversoll

Proofreader: Myckel Anne Phillips

ISBN print: 978-1-947214-35-4

❀ Created with Vellum

This book is dedicated to my oldest daughter who graduated from The College of Veterinary Medicine at Kansas State University, becoming a veterinarian, her life-long dream. While there, we learned of the National Bio and Agro-defense Facility that was being built. You make me proud every day, just by being you.
One of the reasons I chose the subject for this book was to re-visit the little town of Manhattan, Kansas, where she enjoyed four years of her life and we enjoyed many visits.

1

The sun had set over Caspian Lake in Vermont, and Eric Lopez looked up from his book, noticing that the evening shadows had also deepened. Sliding off his reading glasses, no longer able to see the book in his hand, he placed both items on the arm of the Adirondack chair. Sitting on his deck, facing the water, he propped his feet up on the rail and watched as the moon began to rise.

Leaning over, he picked up the glass tumbler he had sat next to him and gave it a slight swirl to mix the water with the Scotch whiskey. Taking a sip, he continued to watch as the moon cast its reflection over the water. He appreciated the view, the quiet of the evening, and the whiskey.

The view was one of the main reasons he had bought the cabin several years ago. It had been strange, having traveled the world for over twenty years in the U.S. Navy—most of those as a SEAL—to begin again, as a civilian, needing to find a place to live. His parents had passed away years before, and his only sibling, his sister, lived near Washington D.C. While he did not mind paying her visits, he had no desire to live in an overcrowded, overpriced metropolis.

When trying to decide where he should purchase a home, he took a map of the United States, closed his eyes, and slapped his finger down on the paper. When he opened his eyes, he saw that his forefinger was pointing at Vermont. With a shrug, he had figured it was as good as any place to settle.

He lucked out when he had found the two-bedroom cabin nestled in five acres of wooded land. The back of his house faced Caspian Lake, and the front was far enough away from the road that it could not be seen. The realtor had extolled the virtues of the upgraded kitchen and bathrooms, as well as the tall stone fire-place in the living room.

Instead, he had walked to the windows near the back, looked out over trees and had appreciated that he could clearly see the lake just behind the property. *I didn't give a shit about the kitchen or bathrooms, but the view...hell, yeah.* Turning around, he had immediately shut her up with the words, "I'll take it."

The quiet atmosphere was another bonus. He could not hear any traffic on the road, nor any neighbors around. Occasionally, on a busy summer day, jet skis and boats carrying noisy vacationers would encroach on his reverie, but where he lived was away from the major vacation spots. The call of birds, the scampering of woodland animals through the leaves, and deer moving through the brush were the only sounds he wanted to hear and, most of the time, that was what he got.

And, of course, the Scotch whiskey. Not a heavy drinker, he had nonetheless acquired the taste for the fine scotch during his SEAL days. At the end of a mission, his team would gather together, pull out whatever glasses they could get their hands on, and pour a splash for each of them. Toasting their success, they sipped the whiskey, enjoying the smokiness and burn. They might go raise hell later but, for a few moments together, they shared a drink.

Sipping the last dregs from his glass, he placed his hands on the arms of his chair and hoisted his body upward. His knee twinged like it always did, but he ignored it as he snagged his tumbler, book, and reading glasses on his way inside. Closing the sliding glass door, he flipped the security bar into place. Setting his alarm by the panel near the door, he moved into the kitchen.

The upgraded kitchen might not have sold him on the home but, after he moved in, he appreciated the work the previous owners had accomplished. Oak cabinets, granite countertops, along with a new stove, dishwasher, and refrigerator. He did not have a gourmet palate, nor did cooking provide great pleasure, but he did like to eat and eat well.

He double checked the windows and front door, security habits long since ingrained still in place. Moving through the bedroom, he continued into the bathroom. Another room that had enjoyed the upgrades from the previous owners, it had been expanded to include a large tiled shower, soaking tub, private toilet, and a double sink. It was a strange habit, but he kept his toiletries to one side of the counter, almost as though a partner would want to use the other sink. But there was no partner, just him.

After a quick shower, he stood at the sink and stared into the mirror. Not the type of man to normally spend much time looking at himself, he felt compelled in that moment to see if he was still the man he used to be.

His body was still muscular, although with a little less bulk. His hair was still mostly black, although now streaked with silver. And, the lines emanating from his eyes were deeper...both from years in the sun and age. *Age...the changer of all.*

Shaking his head, disgusted at the path his mind was wandering down, he brushed his teeth and flipped off the light. The master bedroom was not large but held everything that he needed to be comfortable, just like the rest of the house. He had pondered purchasing a king-sized bed when he moved in, but that would have taken up all the room. So, he settled for a queen-size, giving plenty of space for his chest of drawers and a comfortable chair snuggled into the corner next to a floor lamp.

Climbing into bed, he appreciated the money spent on his firm mattress. Like the rest of him, his back was no longer that of a young man, and he discovered a too-soft mattress gave him no support and, therefore, no sleep. Lying in bed as he did every night, his mind cast back to what many would call the good old days. Men he had served with. Missions he had accomplished—the successful ones, as well as those that were not as successful.

Rolling over, he punched his pillow in an effort to plump it sufficiently. His eyes drifted to the window where he could see the starry night sky above the tree line. With a final sigh, he closed his eyes, willing sleep to come and, as with most nights, it did...eventually.

Early the next morning, Eric rounded the bend near the crystal, blue lake, his feet pounding a steady beat along the path. While landing in Vermont was completely by chance, it was through some research that he decided to live in this part of the state. The clear water of the lake and the surrounding forests gave a sense of peace and tranquility. He could sit on the deck of his cabin and enjoy the view or walk down the path from his home to the edge of the water where he kept his own kayak, which he often ventured out in.

If he gave it much thought, he would acknowledge that it was hard for a former Navy SEAL *not* to live near the water. The desire for an early morning swim, kayaking, or just being able to run along paths that meandered by the lake and through the woods was too strong for him to deny.

He pondered a swim that morning but decided on the run alone. Taking a deep breath of the fresh air, pain suddenly shot through his knee and he stumbled slightly. Forcing his pace to slow, he knew it did not make any sense to push harder than his knee would allow. There was nothing at stake here, no training time to meet, no place to be.

Refusing to focus on the pain, he continued to run along the path that now took him out of the thick evergreens and ran along the lake. In the distance he could see a few of the lodges that were built nearby, but it was too early in the morning for the vacationers to be out and about. With a last look toward the lake, he turned along the path that led back into the forest, appreciating the cool, crisp air that flowed over his body as he continued to run.

As he started the climb up the slight incline toward his cabin, the hairs on the back of his neck stood up. He slowed his pace and deviated from the path. Slipping silently through the forest surrounding his cabin, he made his way to a point where he could see the front of his house. The glint of sunlight off a vehicle's bumper caught his eye. Considering he parked his old pickup truck and SUV in the separate garage, he moved stealthily to gain a better view.

A large, black SUV with tinted windows sat in his driveway, parked near the front door. He observed no movement and was unable to discern anyone sitting inside. Moving around toward the back of his house, he stopped, seeing a man standing on his deck.

Black suit. White dress shirt. Black tie. Dark hair. Sunglasses. *Fuckin' hell.* He hated having his morning routine interrupted and, sure as hell, hated having someone standing on his back deck. But, as he made his way around to the stairs, he had to admit he was curious about his visitor.

Though his eyes were hidden by the sunglasses, it was clear the man was watching his ascent. Making it to the top of his deck, he stood arms akimbo, fists on his hips, and waited. The man did not speak. Neither did he. After a long minute of silence, he huffed out a frustrated breath. *This is bullshit.*

"You want to tell me who you are and why the hell you're standing on my deck?"

He watched as the man slid his sunglasses off before hooking them into his front suit pocket, still without saying a word. Taking the opportunity, he assessed the man fully. They were approximately the same height, both with dark hair streaks with silver, but whereas his stance was poised for the uncertainty of what might come, the other man stood ramrod straight and ease written on his face.

"I don't suppose you'd like to offer me a cup of coffee, would you?" the man finally asked.

He cocked his head to the side and quipped, "Perhaps an introduction might be warranted, before we decide to become best buddies over coffee."

The other man's lips quirked ever so slightly, and Eric was not sure if he was fighting a smile or if that was the best smile he could come up with.

"Branson. Silas Branson."

The man lifted his hand and, after a moment's consideration, Eric stepped forward, clasping it in his own. He had no idea what Silas Branson wanted with him, but with the requisite government vehicle in the front and the formal suit the man wore, he knew it had to be important. Besides, if he had to guess, he was looking at a fellow former SEAL.

With a head jerk to the side, he invited Silas to follow him as he moved through the sliding glass door. Walking toward the kitchen, he called over his shoulder, "Help yourself. Cups are in the cabinet. Coffee's already in the pot. Gimme five. Don't figure you want to have a conversation with me smelling like I do."

With that, he left Silas on his own and headed back to take a shower. Not waiting for the water to warm, he jumped in and rinsed off the sweat. Toweling off, he slid on boxers and jeans and pulled a T-shirt over his body. Scrubbing the towel over his head, he walked back to the living room.

Silas had taken off his suit jacket and it was carefully laid across the back of a chair, a cup of coffee sitting on the coffee table in front of it. The man was standing next to the fireplace, looking at the few framed photographs that he had placed there.

Rounding the kitchen counter, he pulled down his own mug and poured his coffee as well. Taking a sip, he put the mug on the counter and stood facing the living room, his arms in front of him with his palms flat against the surface, taking his weight.

"I don't mean to be a dick," he started, and Silas turned to look at him. "But I don't know you. I trust you enough to invite you into my home and offer you a cup of coffee, but unless you've got something to say to me, I think we can conclude this little meeting right now." He watched as Silas' lips quirked once more.

"Crash."

His brow lowered, but he remained silent.

"My call sign. Crash Branson."

"Ah," he muttered, his eyes widening as he recognized the name. Picking up his cup of coffee, he rounded the counter and motioned toward the chair while sitting down on the sofa. Silas took the silent invitation and sat down as well.

"See you've heard of me."

"Before my time, but yes. You had a fuckin' good reputation as a Lieutenant Commander. Heard you were picked up by Department of Homeland Security." He shrugged slightly and apologized, "'Fraid I didn't hear much after that."

Silas shook his head and waved his hand in a slight dismissive gesture. "Wouldn't have expected you to keep up." He glanced around the small, but comfortable room, before landing on the expansive view outside the window. "You've got a real nice place here. Quiet. Fuckin' gorgeous view. Nice place to retire."

Eric leaned back and settled comfortably. If a former SEAL Lieutenant Commander, now working for DHS, was sitting in his living room, it sure as hell was not about the view. But, Silas did not appear to be in a hurry and, since he had retired, he had nothing but time.

Turning his sharp gaze to him, Silas said, "I heard you helped out with a rescue last month."

That was true. He had been contacted by one of his former teammates who was now working for a private security firm. He had jumped at the chance to assist in a rescue and, having easy access to someone with a helicopter, it had been easy to fly to Boston for the mission.

"Rank—John Rankin was a good SEAL and is a good friend. Works for Lighthouse Security now. I was local, so it was easy to step in and assist."

Silas nodded, and asked, "You ever hear from Preacher?"

"Why do I get the feeling you already know the answers before you ask the questions?"

A slight smile crossed Silas' face. He was referring to Logan "Preacher" Bishop, another one of Eric's SEAL team members and an expert in logistics. Logan had been forced into medical retirement, same as him, several years ago. He had landed in one of the most unpopulated areas in the country—northern Montana —and flew birds for tourists and ski rescues.

He tried to read Silas' face, to judge whether he knew about Preacher's extracurricular activities, but he was not quite sure what to make of the man. And he sure as hell was not going to fill him in.

After another moment of silence, he found that he was no longer interested in playing whatever bullshit games Silas had in mind. "Once again, I don't mean to be a dick, but sitting here shooting the shit with you is not how I was going to spend my morning. I figure you're here for a reason...can we get to it?"

Silas leaned forward and picked up his coffee cup, taking a long sip before setting it back down. Lifting his gaze, he said with a grin, "How do you feel about pigs?"

Pigs? Fuckin' hell.

2

Several minutes later, Eric decided that no guest, even an unexpected one, should have an empty mug. Standing, he snagged Silas' mug off the table, walked back into the kitchen, and refilled their mugs.

Silas had explained that he headed the DHS Secret Division, Bone Frog Command. The concept was simple, while the execution was anything but. His idea was to have retired SEAL commanders plan, coordinate, and lead task force missions. In his opinion, there was no one better equipped to pull a group of people from various agencies into a team.

Eric had to admit, the concept intrigued him. Moving back to the living room, he placed Silas' mug in front of him and retook his seat on the sofa.

"Why me?" he asked, genuinely curious.

"In my experience, SEALs who are forced to retire due to injuries, especially those that are not debilitating, still have a need to serve. And we all know, for those of

11

us in that situation, a regular desk job is not going to cut it." Lifting his shoulders in a shrug, Silas continued, "I have access to the list of former SEAL commanders, and I regularly go through it carefully. When there is a need, I analyze that list and come up with the best person for the job."

He nodded, weighing Silas' words. "I'm listening."

Another slight smile curved Silas' lips, as though he knew Eric was downplaying his interest in order to not look too eager to learn more. "Ever heard of the National Bio and Agro-defense Facility?"

Eyes narrowing, he shook his head. "I know there was an animal disease center on Plum Island in New York. I heard it was shutting down and moving, but that's all I know."

"Yeah, that's right. A branch of DHS ran that lab since 1954. It was originally created to study foot and mouth disease because of the outbreaks in Mexico and Canada. Being surrounded by such a disease was the impetus for creating that center to protect our own country's agriculture. About fifteen years ago, it was decided that Plum Island was no longer the best place to continue that type of biological and agricultural terrorism study. So, a new place was found, almost in the dead center of the United States. Manhattan, Kansas. A small town in the middle of the Kansas prairie, it's only major claim to fame being the home of Kansas State University.

"I know it's been a few years, but you had an under-graduate degree in Biology, so I figure you'll understand the implications of the new center. The new facility researches and develops countermeasures to combat high consequence biological threats involving humans and animals. They are particularly interested in the diseases that can be passed from animals to humans, both here, in the States, and abroad."

"I'm assuming you're getting ready to tell me about the pigs?"

Chuckling, Silas' face finally broke into a grin. "Yeah, we're going to talk about the pigs." Leaning forward, he settled his forearms on his knees with his hands clasped in front of him, keeping his gaze steadily on Eric. "The last major outbreak of a porcine epidemic, in 2014, ran up a cumulative cost of about half a billion dollars."

Eric's eyebrows rose at the number, and Silas continued. "The new facility in Kansas studies all kinds of biological and agricultural diseases. The reason it's run under DHS is because of the implications to our national health and finances. Hell, even you'll remember that there was a bioweapons list found by SEALs in an Afghan cave, handwritten by Al-Qaeda. It wouldn't take much for a foreign entity to infect our animals and bring our country to its knees."

"I'm assuming you've got a new threat coming in?" he asked, his curiosity piqued.

"Couple years ago, the North Korean leader released video footage of one of their biotechnical institutes. They claimed that it was a factory for making pesticides to combat worms and caterpillars that affected their crops. What they didn't realize, is that our people would study that film as intricately as we did. In the background, there was equipment that could be used for the bulk production of live microbes."

"So, on top of the North Koreans being an atomic weapons threat, we're now concerned about them as a biological threat?" He voiced the statement as a question, but he already knew the answer.

"That's right. That shit has hit China and has even found its way into areas of Siberia. Russia is in an uproar, but it's China that will face the biggest impact. Turns out China produces half of all the world's pigs, with over five hundred million swine."

As serious as the discussion was, he stifled a chuckle, realizing he was sitting in his living room sipping coffee with a high-level director of the DHS, and they were discussing fuckin' pigs. Silas lifted his brow, and he apologized. "Sorry."

"Impressed with my knowledge on the porcines of the world?" Silas quipped. "Hell, I didn't even know that pigs were called porcines until this shit started happening."

Unable to hold it in, his chuckle sounded out, soon joined by Silas'. They shared a moment of mirth, before Silas continued.

"If North Korea wants to create a scenario which will literally rock the world's economies, they can develop diseases to be spread amongst farm animals and even between animals and humans."

"I hear what you're saying, but one question still remains—why are you really here?"

"The new facility for the National Bio and Agro-defense Facility is now up and running. They work on and research all types of biological and agricultural diseases and threats vital to our nation's well-being. The DHS is committed to the cause, and that's evident in the facilities fuckin' huge budget. It's been a long time coming, building the facility, and it's been a hard road. There are threats from several places, and have been from the start, but there are two major groups that have the financial backing to potentially make a difference.

"One that we've had our eye on is a local, grassroots group. They started protesting when Manhattan, Kansas was first listed as one of the possibilities for the NBAF. We kept an eye on them but didn't think too much about them because by the time DHS got down to the final six possible places, each of them had a grass-roots group protesting. Obviously, this one has continued. It's taken well over ten years to build this new facility, and they've grown in number and threat in that time."

"I would think the boon to the business growth in that area would be good."

"Yes, but these people say that there are dangerous diseases being studied right in their backyard. They're not wrong, but we have done everything possible to ensure their safety. Still, they claim that if there's a breach in security, they will be the first to be exposed. That won't happen because of the way the facility has been built. Believe me, it's as tight as it can possibly be."

He pondered that for a second, and then asked, "And the other group?"

Silas, whom had barely cracked a smile since entering, actually grimaced. "They are terrorists that parade as an animal rights group. When they started to show significant increases in their funding in a short amount of time, we got suspicious. We've traced the money trail back to Asia but are still working to find out exactly where it originates. Our fear is that, without knowing who they really are, they will manage to infiltrate internally, allowing them to wreak havoc from the inside."

Eric leaned back against the sofa cushions, one ankle resting on the other knee, and considered all he had been told. A familiar sense of expectation moved over him as he attempted to work out exactly what it was Silas wanted him for. Retirement had certainly been relaxing, but he found it more and more difficult to stay mentally engaged. He could run and swim and exercise his body, but he had resorted to reading voraciously to keep his mind active. He found he was relishing the intelligent conversation that had landed directly in his living room and actually looked forward to hearing Silas' proposition.

"We need someone to head to Kansas and work undercover as a journalist touring the NBAF. There is an international science seminar that will soon be held at the facility. While I'm comfortable in the security we have in place, I want someone in there to get a feel for the other journalists in attendance, most of which are international. If you're posing as press, you can get close to the Asian journalists as well as the protesters."

His brows lowered as he pondered what Silas was considering. "That's all you need? Someone to go in and pose as the press in order to keep an eye on the other journalists that are inside and get interviews with the two groups? It hardly sounds like you'd need a former SEAL for that."

"It's more than just that. You'll be analyzing the journalists, ferreting out their intent. Some may genuinely be interested in methods to improve their nation's own response to bioterrorism, but others may be looking for weaknesses to target us later. You're going to need to think quickly, be suspicious, and inconspicious. I want you to pull together a team to assist. You're going to need someone who can handle the logistics. We're going to give you a DHS liaison on the inside. I've also got someone from DHS who's itching to get some field experience, and they're brilliant with surveillance. But, bottom line, we want to know where the biggest threat is coming from. One of those groups? If so, where the fuck are they getting their money? And if any of them have ties to North Korea, we want to know that too. For that kind of intel, I want somebody I can fuckin' trust."

Finished explaining himself, Silas picked up his mug and relaxed back in his chair, allowing Eric time to mull it over. Neither of them said anything for a few minutes as his mind raced. What would keep him from taking the assignment? Certainly nothing here in Vermont. His cabin was easy enough to secure for a few weeks. Certainly not a relationship. He had been married many years before, but his wife divorced him after she found out that being a SEAL wife meant that she was alone often, and it was not as exciting as she thought it would be. In the twenty years since she had left, he had kept relationships to a minimum...usually one night or, occasionally, he might find someone that he would see for a very short period of time.

His gaze moved to Silas who was staring intently back at him, and he let out a breath. "Can't come up with a reason why I shouldn't take this assignment."

Grinning, Silas leaned forward and set his mug on the coffee table before slapping his hands on the arm of the chair and lifting himself up. A slight grimace crossed his face at the movement, an indication that back pain was an ongoing problem.

"Glad to hear it, Eric." He walked over to his suit jacket and pulled out a thumb drive from the inner pocket. Laying it down on the coffee table, he nodded toward it. "That will have the information you need to study about the NBAF, the protesting groups, and basic information about African Swine Fever. That'll make your cover more convincing, as well as give you the inside information you'll need. My office will be in contact through secure methods to fill you in on anything else."

Standing, Eric lifted his arm and they shook hands. "I appreciate you thinking of me for this assignment."

Silas held his gaze for a moment, and then said, "I spend a great deal of time looking for exactly the right person to fulfill a need for the Bone Frog Command. Believe me when I say, you're the man for the job."

He walked him to the front door and stood on his porch as Silas climbed into his SUV with some difficulty. Having his own share of aches and pains, he sympathized with the former SEAL Commander. He continued to watch as Silas pulled out of his driveway, then walked back through the house. Having not had breakfast yet, he quickly scrambled eggs and fried bacon, taking his plate out to the back deck. Sitting in a chair with his feet up on the rail, he ate while enjoying the view of the woods and the lake.

Though he had not studied the information on the thumb drive yet, his mind already rolled to the assignment at hand. A slow smile curved his lips at the idea of a new mission once again. It sounded easy. Go in as a journalist, interview some protesting groups, keep an eye on the foreign journalists...*easy*.

3

Eric sat in his first-class seat on the airplane flying to Kansas City, his eyes closed. His headphones served the purpose of keeping his seatmate from talking to him while he tried to get some rest. He had spent the past week pouring over all of the information that Silas had provided to him. He had learned as much as he could about the NBAF and, he had to admit, he was impressed with both the facility and its scope. He had also studied many of the various diseases that they sought to prevent, find cures for, or eradicate, so that he had at least a layman's idea of what kinds of questions a journalist might ask.

He had also gotten in touch with his old SEAL buddy, Logan Bishop, but it was Logan's wife he spent most of his time talking to. Vivian Bishop had been a biologist with the DHS and had met Logan when they worked on a mission together rooting out a terrorist cell in Alaska. She had left DHS when she married

Logan and settled into his home in Montana. She now worked as a biology college professor and advisor to DHS. She had graciously answered the numerous questions he had plied her with.

Silas had been right—his Biology degree from years ago had come in handy but, like a lot of previous education, he had forgotten much. Vivian was a great resource, helping him understand some of the information he was reviewing. She promised she was only a phone call away if he got stuck and needed help and, with Logan's ability to ensure their communication was secure, he was comfortable taking her up on her offer.

The pilot made the announcement that they would soon be landing at the airport in Kansas City, and he slipped off his headphones, placing them in his carry-on luggage. Exiting the plane shortly thereafter, he realized that the airport was small, so it took him little time to collect his luggage and step outside.

He barely had time to look at his phone for his contact, when he heard his name being called. Looking up, he watched as a tall, gangly, young man with a wide smile and bright red hair came bounding over.

"Eric? Right? I am right, aren't I?"

Preferring a subtler greeting, he nodded. "And you are?"

"Chris. Chris Peterson." His brow crinkled in thought, and he asked, "Aren't you expecting me?"

"Yes, I was expecting to meet Chris Peterson," he said, "but not to have my name shouted across the airport."

Chris blushed, the pink on his cheeks somehow

blending into the red of his hair. "Sorry! All this is kinda new to me, but I can't tell you how excited I am."

Not replying, he bent to grab his suitcase with one hand, while keeping his briefcase in the other. Staring pointedly at Chris, he waited to see which direction they would go in. Chris continued to look at him, smiling widely, until Eric finally said, "You did drive here? There is actually an automobile that we're going to be heading to, right?"

Chris startled out of his obvious admiration and blushed again. "Oh, right. Yeah." His gaze dropped down to the suitcase in Eric hand, and he asked, "Uh, you want me to get that?"

With a jerky shake of his head, he replied, "Nope. You're not here to be my personal valet. But, right now, you are supposed to be my driver, so if we could get going, that'd be great."

Smiling again, Chris turned and led him over to a red Jeep Cherokee. Throwing open the back door, he stood back while Eric settled his cases inside, then shut the door. They both climbed into the front seat and Chris pulled out of the airport parking. It only took a moment for Eric to merge onto the highway, heading south to I-70, which he knew cut across Kansas and would take them directly to Manhattan.

"It's not usually so crowded on the highway," Chris said. "But you got here at rush hour."

Eric glanced around at the wide highway, the amount of traffic minimal, and wondered for a second if Chris was joking. "Are you from around here?"

Chris nodded, still smiling, and replied, "Born and

raised right here. Got my degree in cybersecurity and was able to get on with DHS after graduation." His blue eyes crinkled as he grinned wider, and added, "They learned I have a proclivity for not only figuring out cybersecurity, but how to get around it when I need to." He looked at him from the corner of his eye, and added, "But this is the first time I've been on a real case...you know, where I'm actually in the action."

He had been staring out the windshield, wondering what Chris would think about rush-hour traffic on the East Coast, but he now slid his gaze to the side and stared at Chris, seeing the enthusiasm written plainly on the young man's face.

"You do know this is mostly a fact-finding operation to begin with, right? I don't see it as a go-in-with-guns-blazing ordeal."

"Yeah, yeah, I know," Chris said, his smile dropping from his face. "I get that it probably won't be all that exciting, but it's still my first chance to actually do something besides just sit in an office and putter with the computer."

He nodded, expecting the conversation to be over, but Chris continued with his running monologue. "I got you booked into one of the hotels near the NBAF. They have one of those king-size bed suites that has more room, so I figured you'd like that. Also, breakfast is included with the price of the room, and it's a pretty good one. Not like just cereal and bananas. I went by to check it out and they've got scrambled eggs, sausage, bacon, biscuits and gravy, and a big ol' tray of all kinds of pastries. 'Course, they got juice and coffee and milk, too."

Part of him wanted to lean his head back against the headrest and close his eyes, but Eric found himself enjoying the Kansas vista as they merged onto I-70 too much to do so. Plus, if he were honest with himself, there was something about Chris' enthusiasm that kept his attention.

So, for the next two hours, Chris talked about Kansas ranches—something he was well acquainted with since he had been raised on one. As the young man droned on, Eric took in the plains, prairies, and rolling hills. The only major city they went through was Topeka, and it only took a few minutes to get from one side to the other on the highway.

Finally, Chris turned off of the highway and onto a smaller road leading north to Manhattan. As they got closer, he announced, "Manhattan, Kansas. Home of the Kansas State Wildcats. This little town bleeds purple, especially during football season. It's also known as the Little Apple." He laughed, and said, "Get it? Manhattan...Little Apple? You know, since Manhattan, New York is called The Big Apple, this place got the nickname Little Apple. Isn't that a hoot?"

Eric's lips curved into a smile in spite of his best effort to maintain closed off. He had already read that Manhattan, Kansas was known by that nickname, but hearing it from Chris added to his amusement.

Chris' face settled into a more serious expression, and he said, "Look over to the left, and you can see the NBAF."

He leaned forward and looked out the window, recognizing the outer buildings from all the information he had read. Nondescript, neat, sprawling buildings behind a tall fence. He knew there was much more to the facility than met the eye but remained silent as he stared.

With a nod, he said, "Thanks. You can take me to the hotel now."

Once there, he got settled and watched as Chris turned from gangly, goofy, geeky, young man into a serious agent in training. Chris opened up a case that he had brought with him and quickly began scanning the room for any audio or visual bugs.

Declaring the room clean after his sweep, Chris then began setting up his own surveillance to keep an eye out in case anyone came into the room. Eric had to admit, he was impressed. Once Chris was finished, they sat down, he in the chair on one side of the coffee table while Chris sprawled on the sofa.

He began, "I'm assuming you've been briefed on everything that I'm going to be doing. I have already set up two separate interviews, one with each of the protesting groups. Undetectable audio and visual recording need to be on me. I don't want to make any assumptions that the local one is not sophisticated, but from what I've read, they probably won't be expecting me to have anything. They're excited about getting press, so I think that won't be a problem. The other one? I could easily see them being much more suspicious of someone coming in to interview them."

Chris leaned forward, his forearms on his knees and

nodded enthusiastically. "That's what I was told." Sliding his case over, he flipped it open. "I wasn't sure what you'd be wearing for the interviews, so I've got something that goes with a tie, in case you're wearing a suit jacket. If you're going for the more casual look, I've got something that can attach to glasses. Of course, you can use that with a suit and tie as well. I just wanted to give you a choice."

"Glasses? I wear them for reading, but—"

"I've got some," Chris said, while simultaneously shoving his glasses up on his nose. Reaching into his case again he brought out a pair of fashionable eyeglasses and laid them on the table. "Since you wear reading glasses, these will be easy for you to get used to."

"I'll use the glasses." he said, picking them up to look them over. "In case anyone is checking into me, then they'll always see me with the glasses on and won't think anything of it."

"Got it," Chris said, taking the glasses from him and setting them to the side. "I'll have everything ready for you as soon as I double check all my equipment and connections." Reaching into his case again, he said, "I've worked on your press badge, the special one that only the press allowed to go into the NBAF will have. The head honcho will know that you're coming in, and this badge will allow you to get in without any problems. I've also got a microchip embedded in it, so that I'll know where you are at any given time once you're inside."

Listening to Chris explain everything, he realized it

was the first time that he had ever worked with someone who was not already part of his team. Someone that he knew. Someone that he trusted. While Chris continued to tinker with some of the things that he was bringing out of his case, he leaned back in his chair and stared.

In the field, on a mission, trust was everything. He trusted his SEAL brothers, but this was different. He knew Chris had been vetted by Silas. He knew Chris would have the tools and toys necessary. *But would he have the instinct?* Uncertain of the answer to that question, he continued to watch, praying that nothing went wrong with the mission but, knowing if it did, Chris had better have his six.

4

Lydia Hughes, her brown, wavy hair pulled up into a sloppy bun on top of her head, slipped on protective gloves before walking into the room. She was dressed in her usual blue scrubs, with her pants tucked into high, white, rubber boots. As she moved about the occupants, she was greeted enthusiastically. Snorts. Grunts. Squeals. Grinning widely, she bent over and rubbed her hand along the backs of several of her audience members, scratching behind their ears.

She had never intended to work with pigs when she first began her doctorate in veterinary medicine, but life had a way of taking its own course, and sometimes she found the easiest thing to do was follow the flow. When she had completed her internship at the VetMed School at KSU, her daughter wanted to stay in Kansas to finish high school. The NBAF had opened and needed veterinarians as one of their many employees. They offered a fabulous salary and tremendous benefits, so she jumped at the chance.

"Lydia!"

Turning, she watched a young woman dressed in the same outfit that she was wearing, open the gate and step into the pen. "Good morning, Beth," she called out. Looking just behind her, she also greeted Jim, as he walked in.

Beth was a senior veterinary student at the Kansas Veterinary Medicine School at KSU, who had the fortunate opportunity to be able to work part-time at NBAF, due to both her parents having security clearances working for the government. Jim had already earned his DVM and had been accepted for a year internship to work under her.

Every day, they made their inspection rounds first thing in the morning and in the middle of the afternoon. They had worked together for several months, easily falling into a routine. Beth bent and scooped up a piglet in her arms and held it tightly for Lydia to examine.

She lifted up each of the ears, calling out the tag number to Jim, who stood nearby with his tablet. She checked the pig's snout, making sure it was moist but with no discharge and rubbed her hands along its skin, checking to make sure there were no wounds or sores. As she verbalized her observations during the exam, Jim made notations by the pig's number.

When Lydia's exam of that piglet was complete, Beth placed the wiggling, squealing animal back to the floor, before snagging the next one. As they moved on to the larger pigs, it took another hour for them to complete their task. Once finished, they left the pen, securing it tightly before moving to the area just outside the animal enclosure.

Lydia led the way, moving to the concrete slab underneath a shower hose. Grabbing the hose, she washed the muck off her boots before handing the hose to Beth. Stepping out of her boots, she placed them on the drainage rack before sliding on her shoes.

As Beth and Jim followed her steps, she tossed her gloves into the trash and walked over to the sink. With her sleeves rolled up, she scrubbed her hands and forearms with the precision of a surgeon.

It did not matter that she had been dealing with healthy animals, everyone at NBAF had to follow the same protocol. She did not mind, since it was for her safety as well as the safety of others.

As Beth and Jim cleaned up, Lydia sat at her desk and pulled up the latest information that Jim had entered. She found no change in any of the piglets, something she was very pleased about. For the next hour, they worked on their various reports, the conversation light amongst them.

"How's Caroline?" Beth asked.

She smiled. "She's good. Settled into her dorm and told me that she got most of the classes she wanted. So far, she likes her roommate."

Beth snorted, and said, "That'll last about another month. Then, they'll probably be at each other's throats."

"Honest to God, Beth," Jim said, sitting over at his

desk. "I swear that's a girl thing. Guys can go off to college and get along with anybody. Messy, neat, loud, quiet. Just doesn't seem to matter to guys."

Beth turned around, planting her hands on her hips. "I don't believe that, Jim. You were a college freshman, what? Eight years ago? I'll bet your freshman roommate got on your last nerve also."

Jim looked over at Beth and laughed. "Actually, no. Within the first month, he fell madly, deeply in love and moved in with his girlfriend. I ended up having the room completely to myself." With a wink toward Lydia, he said, "Hope for your sake, that doesn't happen to Caroline and she ends up with her roommate's boyfriend living in their room for the rest of the year."

Eyebrows raised to her forehead, she shook her head. "Hmmm, maybe I'd better call Caroline and warn her that she'd better not let her roommate walk all over her!"

Beth laughed, and said, "Speaking of romance, don't forget, you're going out with a couple of us tonight to celebrate Penny's engagement."

Her shoulders slumped at the reminder. "Why on earth did I agree to go out tonight? All the bars are filled with very young college students."

Beth rolled her eyes, "Lydia, you're hardly old!" Looking over at the clock, she said, "I'm out of here. Remember to meet us at eight o'clock." She bolted out the door, leaving Lydia frowning, still sitting at her desk.

Jim looked over, sympathy in his eyes. "She's right, you know. You're not old. But, thank God, you're also not twenty-two. Nothing more irritating than somebody being that young and so sure about everything." Shutting down his computer, he stood and stretched before heading to the door. "I'm off the clock too. Don't work late."

She finished the report she was working on before closing up the office. Walking down the hall, she gave a nod toward her supervisor, Paul, who was busy in a conversation with Dr. Linda Hughley, one of the NBAF directors and a world expert on certain porcine diseases. Finishing his conversation, he turned to her just as she was almost to the door.

"Lydia, a moment please."

She turned and walked back to him, looking up expectantly.

"Our section will be part of the international press tour. We will have some of the journalists in this week to take a look around, while the scientists will be in the research area. I will leave you in charge of their tour."

Stunned, she asked, "What on earth am I supposed to show them? Right now, I'm spending all my time with the swine in preparation for the studies next month."

Waving his hand dismissively, he replied, "That's fine. There's only a small delegation of journalists that are coming through. The scientists they are accompanying are interested in the African Swine Fever prevention. You can go over your job and some of the research that occurs at this facility. That's all you need to do."

He did not give her a chance to respond, turning on his heels and walking back down the hall. Sighing, she made her way to the outside door, sliding her badge over the security reader. She hated the idea of speaking to journalists, knowing that her every word could be quoted. Confident in her job and her abilities, she nonetheless dreaded being on display.

A few minutes later, driving home, her mind rolled to the evening. Not sure what to wear, she wished that she was staying in and watching TV with a nice cup of tea, instead of going to a bar that would be filled with a bunch of people her daughter's age. *God, I feel old.*

Eric and Chris went to get a rental car, so that Eric would have transportation while there. Once back at the hotel, Chris headed to his own room, leaving Eric a chance to review his notes. It was not long before his stomach started to grumble. Desiring to find a place to eat dinner before turning in early, he asked Chris for some recommendations, knowing that Chris had been in Manhattan before.

After GPSing locations, he noted that several were within walking distance of the hotel. He decided to check them out and stop at whichever looked good. He walked past a few chain restaurants, whose parking lots were filled with family minivans, and quickly nixed those. Continuing down the road, a little closer to campus, he stepped into one that looked decent and made his way to the bar.

Ordering a buffalo burger and fries, he sipped his beer while casting his gaze around the crowded room. Some people, like him, were eating, but it appeared that many were there just for the drinks. As it got darker outside, the music seemed to get louder, as did the shouts from the people around.

Once served, he made short work of his dinner, nodding toward the bartender as he got another beer. He twisted around on his barstool and wondered how many of the young people there were barely of drinking age.

A few girls sidled up to him, the blatant sexual offers not even close to being subtle. Their bodies were tanned and toned. Their breasts were pert. Their dresses were tight, some almost looking like they were made out of a brightly colored latex condom. That strange analogy gave him pause, and he shook his head and turned back to his beer. There was nothing about them that caught his interest. *God, I feel old.*

His elbow was bumped slightly, and as he jerked his head around, he heard a soft voice say, "I'm so sorry. Please excuse me."

The voice was not only soft, but slightly deep, with a sultry edge to it. Not a girl's voice...a woman's voice. Catching her eyes, he was speechless for a moment. Standing next to him was definitely a woman. Her thick, dark hair hung to just below her shoulders, trimmed so that the edges flipped slightly. Her brown eyes were warm, with little flecks of amber that caught the lights from behind the bar. Her makeup had been applied with a light touch, and her lips were kissed with a rosy gloss.

A dark green, knit shirt showed no cleavage but gave evidence to her curves. His eyes swept downward, and he admired the way her ass was showcased in her dark jeans. Wearing low heeled boots, he estimated her height as just tall enough to tuck under his chin if he was standing.

He blinked as she smiled his way and, while he could categorize and appreciate her assets, she was of indeterminate age, so he let his thoughts stop there. Then again, her face was beautiful and youthful but exuded maturity. She was definitely not one of the coeds that crowded the bar.

Her smile faltered, and he realized that he had not accepted her apology for bumping into him. Her eyes dropped and she began to turn away.

"You don't need to apologize," he said. "This place is pretty packed. It would be hard not to bump into someone here." He held his breath for a second, releasing it when she turned back around and greeted him with her beautiful smile once again.

She cocked her head to the side, and said, "I agree, this place really is crowded. It's not something that I typically do, but I was invited out this evening, so here I am."

Suddenly interested in talking to her more, he nodded toward the empty bar stool that was next to him, and asked, "Would you like to join me? Or do you need to get back to your friends?"

Shaking her head, her hair gently floating about her shoulders, she replied, "It was an engagement party for a coworker, not a close friend. I've made my appearance and wished them well. I was actually getting ready to leave, when someone bumped into me, and I, in turn, bumped into you."

Returning her smile, he said, "I'd love to buy you a drink." He watched her hesitate, then once again breathed easier when she nodded and placed her hand in his. He assisted her onto the barstool and signaled for the bartender.

"I'll just have a glass of white…Riesling, if you have it."

Within a minute, the bartender returned with her glass of wine and she took a sip, before turning and looking at him. "I'm Lydia."

"Eric. Pleased to meet you."

Tilting her head to the side, she asked, "Do you live here?"

Shaking his head, he replied, "No. I'm here on business. What about you?"

She nodded and smiled. "Live here. Work here."

Small talk ensued, but it became harder and harder to hear. Their knees had moved closer together, and as the noise in the bar increased, their heads inclined toward each other.

Spying her empty wine glass, he confessed, "I'd love to offer you another drink, but this place is getting more than I can handle."

Nodding, she agreed. "I understand. It was very nice meeting you—"

"Whoa, whoa," he rushed. "I'm not trying to get rid of you, but I thought that we could go somewhere else. Since I don't know the area, is there another place that we could go to have a drink that's a little less…manic?"

She threw her head back and laughed, and he watched, thoroughly enjoying her mirth. Not a giggle or a coy simper but a full-throated sound of enjoyment. An image of the two of them finding a more physical type of enjoyment flew through his head, and he shifted slightly as his cock twitched.

She lowered her head and held his gaze. "Manic is exactly the right word for this place. I'd love to continue our conversation and have a drink somewhere else."

He slid off the stool after throwing a wad of bills onto the bar, plenty to cover his dinner and their drinks. Offering his hand again, he loved the feeling as she placed hers in his, and he assisted her off the stool. Just as he had imagined, the top of her head came to right under his chin.

She had not removed her hand from his, and he continued to hold it firmly as they made their way through the crowd to the door. Once outside, with the door closed behind them, the din was muffled.

"Oh, my goodness. I feel like I can think now that it's less noisy."

He agreed, then asked, "Where do you suggest we go?"

"There's a little Italian restaurant not too far from here. They have wonderful desserts and offer a wide variety of beer and wine." She smiled up at him, and added, "And, it's quiet."

Offering his elbow, he said, "Then, Lydia, it sounds perfect." She did not make him wait, instantly sliding her hand into the crook of his elbow and leading them down the sidewalk.

5

Lydia stared at the man sitting across from her in the back, corner table of the Italian restaurant. After the noise of the bar they had come from, the soft music playing, and the low voices of the other patrons were a welcome respite.

She had been surprised by the attraction she felt for him from the first minute he turned his dark-eyed gaze toward her. Not one to pick up a man in a bar…or be picked up…she nonetheless had felt a strange pull toward him.

She liked his gentle voice and calm manner. She liked the way he stared at her face when she spoke, instead of letting his eyes wander or settle on her breasts. She liked the easy conversation and the way his eyes crinkled at the sides when he laughed. And she would be a liar if she did not admit the fact that he was drop-dead gorgeous. Black hair shot through with silver. Tall, with a muscular body. His navy blue shirt emphasized his chest and arms and his jeans emphasized everything that she was trying hard not to notice. *When was the last time I had sex? When was the last time I was seriously interested in thinking of having sex with someone?*

She calculated the answer to that silent question in her head and was surprised when she realized that it had been a couple of years. A fellow doctorate student, close to graduation, and both needing a release. That was all it had been but, now, with her current dinner companion, she was tingling in places she had not forgotten but had definitely ignored.

She remembered the conversation she had with Caroline a few months ago, where her daughter encouraged her to get out and "get some". Determined *not* to continue that conversation, she had immediately looked at her daughter, and said, "I'm more concerned about you and safe sex than me and safe sex." Caroline had laughed, and quipped, "Mom, for you to practice safe sex means that you need to actually *have* sex."

Now, she was sitting across from the first man she had been interested in in a long time and finding it hard to focus on his words when electricity was zapping between them.

The shared tiramisu had been decimated and their wine glasses were now empty. They had chatted easily, without delving into too much personal information. She wanted it that way, having no desire to open herself up to deep scrutiny. Men usually thought she was younger than she was but, at thirty-seven years old, she was hardly ancient.

Of course, when a man found out that she had a child when she was only eighteen, that tended to steer the conversation in a direction she did not want to go. So far, Eric had not asked questions that were too personal, keeping the conversation light. He did not wear a wedding band, and his ring finger did not appear to be a different shade of tan than his other fingers, indicating that he had not simply slipped off his wedding ring before going out this evening.

"Lydia?"

Blinking out of her reverie, she had missed what he had said. The heat of blush rushed over her face, and she said, "Oh, Eric, I'm so sorry. My mind wandered, but I assure you that it had nothing to do with you." Before he had a chance to speak, she added, "I mean, it did have to do with you, but not being bored with what you were saying. I was thinking of you, but just not… oh, dear. I seem to be babbling."

His smile widened as a deep chuckle sent shivers over her. He reached across the table and placed his hand on hers, gently squeezing her fingers. "I had only said that I was having a really good evening. I left the hotel hours ago in search of a place to get something to eat, never imagining that I would meet someone so charming."

She turned her hand over so that her palm was up, and they linked fingers. Her breath caught in her throat as the feel of his hand on hers sent desire pooling deep inside. Sucking in a quick breath, she rushed, "The evening doesn't have to end, if you don't want it to. I know that seems very forward, but you can take the offer or leave it, as you feel." As the words left her mouth, she wished she could pull them back, but they were already out there, sizzling between them like the current that had been present ever since she met him.

He stared at her, and she felt her cheeks heat with blush. "I don't normally do this—"

"I can tell," he hurried to assure. "I've thoroughly enjoyed this evening and wondered if there was any way it would keep going. I just didn't know how to bring it up but am thrilled that you did."

"I almost didn't," she admitted, her lips curving.

Smiling, he said, "I can't think of anything more I'd rather do than have more time with you. I'm staying at a hotel not too far from here. I walked to the bar, so I don't have my car—"

"I parked just down the street from the bar," she inserted. "We can walk back and then can drive to your hotel."

He had already paid their bill, so he stood quickly with her hand still in his. Pulling her gently to her feet, he wrapped his arm around her and guided her back out onto the sidewalk. It only took a few minutes to walk back to where her car was parked, and he held out his hand for the keys.

Unused to someone else driving her car, she hesitated. Tilting her head to the side, she asked, "Are you the type of man who feels like a woman can't drive you?"

He turned and faced her, stepping closer. Her back

was against her car, and his hands moved to either side, enveloping her in his warmth. He moved his face closer, stopping when his lips were only a whisper away from hers. "I have no problem with the woman being in the driver seat," he replied. "But, for tonight, I find myself wanting to take care of you. Will you let me do that?"

Holding his gaze, she had barely nodded when he moved in, his lips finding hers. The kiss began light, slow and smooth, but as a small groan slipped from deep within herself, the kiss flamed hot. She lifted her hands, placing her palms on his chest. His heartbeat pounded through her fingertips, and she gasped as he slid one hand to the back of her head, angling her mouth for maximum pleasure.

His tongue slipped through her open lips, and she felt her knees weaken at the sensations rushing through her. Forgetting everything else, she answered back with her own tongue, tangling it with his. Her hands slipped from his chest to around his waist, and she pulled her body flush to his. Lost in the kiss, she blinked at the sudden feeling of cool air between them.

Pushing off of the car, he separated from her body an inch, dragging a ragged breath deep into his lungs. "Damn, Lydia. Let's get back to my place."

She placed her car keys in his hand and smiled as he opened the passenger door. He rounded the front quickly, pushed her seat back to accommodate his long legs, and fired up the engine.

They were back at his hotel within a couple of minutes, and he escorted her to his room.

She barely had time to register that his hotel room

was larger than the average room, with a king-size bed, a separate sitting area including a sofa and chair, and a door leading to what she could ascertain was the bathroom. Once inside, he closed the door and whirled her around to face him.

They stared at each other for a few seconds, the sexual energy zapping around the room, filling her with something she had not experienced in a long time.

Suddenly, as though the starting gun of a race had gone off, they lunged at each other, becoming a tangle of arms and clothes, mouths, and kisses. Her shirt was whipped over her head as she grappled with his. She managed to get her hands up under his shirt and over his tight, muscular abs, then groaned when she was unable to push it up higher. Their lips separated just enough for him to reach behind him, grab the back of the material and pull it over his head. Now able to have her hands on his entire torso, she felt his warm, strong skin underneath her fingertips.

As she stood in her bra, the mounds of her breasts plumping over the tops of the satin, he slammed his lips back down on hers before kissing his way down her neck. Bending, his kisses continued until he latched onto her nipple through the material, sucking hard. Her fingers slid up from his back to his head as she held him to her breast, her fingernails dragging slightly over his scalp.

Wanting to feel his lips on her skin, she brought her hands to the front and quickly unsnapped her bra, her breasts jiggling with the movement of shaking the straps off her shoulders. He quickly accommodated, his mouth sucking one nipple while his fingers pinched the other.

As if on cue, their hands both moved to their jeans, quickly unzipping and shucking the material down their legs. Her left hand grasped onto his shoulder as she bent to take off her boots. Once she had accomplished that, she kicked off her jeans.

Standing, she realized he was naked, and she had only her panties on, but he bent and hooked his thumbs into the satin, pulling them down her legs as well.

Now completely naked, she was suddenly nervous. Her breasts were full, their weight keeping them from being as pert as someone much younger and smaller. Her waist was trim, but she knew her abdomen had the slight, white remnants of stretch marks from when she carried Caroline. Her hips were full, and as she stared at his amazingly toned body, she wished that she had not given up on her crunches and runs.

Her gaze dropped to the movement of his hand fisting his cock. Suddenly, wanting to feel the pressure of his body on top of hers and that magnificent cock moving inside her, all thoughts of her body's imperfections flew out of her mind. With a slow smile, she backed to the bed, then sat and stretched back. Leaning up on her elbows, she whispered, "Please."

He looked at her with such adoration, she had never felt more beautiful. "Lydia, that's one thing you don't have to do. You do not have to beg." He placed one knee on the bed, before crawling over her body, straddling her thighs. The scent of her arousal filled the air and he bent to suckle each breast. Her fingers clutched his head as her hips lifted up feeling his erection pressing into her.

Scooting back down her body, he lifted one of her legs, opening her to him. After placing a kiss on her stomach, he moved his lips over her mound before latching onto her clit. Inserting a finger into her sex, he sucked and nipped until her inner muscles clenched.

She clapped her hand over her mouth to stifle the sounds coming from deep inside as her orgasm sent shivers throughout her body. She lay sated, barely aware as he lifted himself back over her. Her eyelids fluttered open, and she could feel the heat of blush from her breasts all the way up to her hairline. "God, that was embarrassing," she moaned.

Eyebrows lifting, he held his face just over hers, and asked, "Embarrassing? I thought it was fuckin' amazing."

She held his gaze and honesty won out over attempting to be coy. "That was quick, so I guess you can figure that it's been a long time for me."

He slid his nose along hers before planting a sweet kiss on her lips. "I'm honored that someone as beautiful and nice as you wanted to give yourself to me," he admitted. "But knowing that it's been a while for you, I'm even more honored that you're sharing this with me."

She had expected a cocky reply from him, but his words touched her. Her lips curved in a slight smile, and she slid her hands from his back, up and over his shoulders. "If that was just the appetizer, I can't wait till we get to the meal."

Laughing, he said, "Babe, I promise you're going to get all seven courses, including dessert."

Leaning to the side, Eric snagged the condom packet he had tossed to the bed before his jeans had hit the floor. Ripping it open, he rolled the condom over his eager cock. Shifting his hips between Lydia's thighs, he held his upper body off of her chest with his forearms planted on either side of her and placed his tip at her entrance. Knowing it had been a while for her, he eased his way in, allowing her body to adjust.

They may have been strangers, but their bodies quickly adapted to the rhythm of his thrusts. The friction was beginning to short-wire his brain, and he wondered how long he would last. Her hands were moving from the small of his back up to his neck and down again, her nails dragging lightly over his sensitive skin. Her legs were wide as her heels dug into his tight ass, and he groaned, "Are you close? Please, God, be close."

A chuckle sounded from deep inside Lydia at Eric's plea. She felt the coil inside tighten and, while his fingers and lips had been wonderful, his cock was reaching places that were sending her closer to a more powerful and stimulating climax. "Yes," she breathed.

Suddenly, she felt her body tighten around him, but this time she was unable to hold back calling out his name as her orgasm sent ripples of pleasure throughout her body. Immediately, he threw his head back, his face red as he continued to thrust and power through his release.

Once every drop was wrung from him, he plopped

to the bed, barely shifting to keep from landing on top of her. For several minutes, they lay, arms and legs tangled, bodies sweaty, breaths ragged, and heartbeats pounding. Finally recovering, he did not want to move, but knew he needed to dispose of the condom.

Mumbling, "Be right back," he headed to the bathroom.

She lay for a minute, satisfied, and wondered what the protocol should be. She sat up and began to scoot to the edge of the bed, when he walked back into the room. She stood as he approached, their naked bodies now familiar to each other. Starting to reach for her clothes on the floor, his hand grabbed hold of her arms gently, stilling her movements.

She lifted her gaze to him, and he said, "Will you stay with me?"

She smiled, a light blush crossing her cheeks. Nodding slowly, giving his question great consideration, she replied, "Yes, I'll stay. I'd like that."

She moved to the bathroom, and after a few minutes of taking care of her business, she walked back out into the bedroom. He had on his boxers but handed her one of his clean T-shirts.

"I wasn't sure if you preferred to have something to sleep in," he said.

She took the proffered shirt and pulled it on. Crawling under the covers, she snuggled up next to him as he wrapped his arms tightly around her. Uncertain if she should say anything, she remained quiet and so did he. At first, it seemed awkward, and then she realized it really was simply comfortable. She did not need him to tell her that it had been great, and she did not need to ask if she would see him again.

So, snuggling into his embrace, she let sleep overtake her.

———

Asking her to stay had surprised Eric. He normally wanted the evening to be over as soon as both parties had been satisfied. But she was different, and he found himself wanting to climb back in bed with her and hope that, maybe, there would be a round two sometime before sunrise. Not used to sharing his bed with a woman for sleep, he was glad that she had not started talking, trying to analyze what they had. Brushing her hair from her face, he stared as her body grew heavy, knowing sleep had finally claimed her. His heart knew that it had been special, but he also knew he was only there for a very short while and needed to keep his mind on the mission. Even if it had only been for a night, he could not help but think, *What if?*

———

In the early morning, before the sun rose, Lydia slipped from the bed. As quietly as possible, she grabbed her clothes and moved into the bathroom to dress. Looking down at Eric's T-shirt, her fingers clutched the material, warring with the desire to take it with her as a reminder. Finally, shaking her head, she knew she did not need a tangible reminder of the wonderful night.

Folding it carefully, she laid it on the bed as she took one last look at him. He appeared younger when he was sleeping, his face relaxed. With a smile, and a slightly heavy heart, she turned and slipped out of the room. As she drove the short distance across town to her rented home, she could not help but think, *What if?*

6

Two days later, Eric sat in the parking lot of the NBAF and took a moment to survey the front of the building. It appeared the employee parking lot was to the side, although many employees were entering through a security gate near the front.

A small group of protesters, holding hand-painted signs declaring 'No NBAF' and wearing white T-shirts with the same words emblazoned across the front, were standing near the front gate. He recognized Chester Thompson, the leader of the local protesting group.

Alighting from his rental car, he weaved through the automobiles in the parking lot and made his way to the front. The group was milling about, a few shouting the occasional chant but most just waving their signs. The employees that were going through that entrance chatted amongst themselves, paying no attention to the group protesting.

To a bystander, the small protesting group

appeared innocuous. Twelve men and women standing around sipping their coffee, doing nothing more than being a fixture at best, background noise at worst. But, to someone who had served as a SEAL in Afghanistan and other locations around the world, he knew that there was danger in assuming they were harmless. A few of the worst terrorists that he had come up against had been banal in both appearance and early actions.

Assuring that his press badge was hanging about his neck, he adjusted his glasses as he walked toward the group. No one paid any attention to him until he moved closer. A few of the protesters glanced at him, their brows furrowing before their eyes dropped to the badge proclaiming him a journalist. Then, welcoming smiles appeared on their faces.

"Good morning," he called out. "Looks like a beautiful morning here in Kansas."

Murmurings of greetings met his ears, and out of his peripheral vision he noticed Chester had turned around and was eyeing him carefully.

Smiling widely, he exclaimed, "I'm here to do some interviewing, and I set up an interview with someone named Chester. Thought I'd see if he was here today, just to go ahead and meet him."

A woman stepped forward, her gray hair chopped in a short bob that did little to flatter her round face. Her white T-shirt stretched tightly across her figure, and her feet were encased in boots that looked better suited for a farm than standing for long periods of time on a sidewalk. "You'd be wanting to talk to Chester Thompson," she indicated the man in question with a hand toss toward the side. "He handles all our press."

Offering her up smile and nod, Eric said, "Appreciate it. Thank you." As he turned toward Chester, he noticed the man's eyes raked him from top to bottom before coming back and resting on his face. Moving closer, he stuck out his hand, and said, "You must be Chester. I'm Eric Lopez, with the International Scientific Press Corps."

Chester did not offer a wide smile in return, but he took Eric's hand and gave it a firm shake. Eric knew he was being assessed and found it interesting that the local rancher would be so suspicious.

"I'm Chester Thompson, as Julie over there mentioned."

"Good to meet you. I understand that you're the leader of this group?"

"I have that honor," Chester replied. "Our numbers may be small, but our desire to make sure our lands are safe is just as big as it ever was."

Nodding enthusiastically, he said, "I made contact with you last week, so that we can discuss your cares and concerns. I'm very interested in interviewing you and your group."

Chester's eyes dropped down to the badge on his chest once more, and he said, "Aren't you here just to get your tour where the bigwigs inside tell you that this is all for the good of America?"

"Yes, sir, I am here for that. But I want to tell the whole story. I don't want to just take what these people in here tell me and believe it's gospel. I want to make sure that I have a chance to hear all sides of what's going on here, and I believe that you're the person that can give me that perspective."

Chester nodded, his eyes less suspicious than when he first approached. He noticed the others in the group seemed to take their instruction from Chester, even if it was just his nonverbal communication. As Chester relaxed, the others seemed to as well.

"Is there a good time that we could meet?" he asked.

Chester lifted his hand and rubbed his chin for a moment, then offered, "You're more than welcome to come out to my place. "

Surprised at the invitation, he pulled out his phone and looked up expectantly. "If you give me your address, we can set up a time."

Chester rattled it off, then said, "If you want to come for lunch, my wife's a good cook."

Pleased that it had been so easy to get the interview set up, he nodded enthusiastically, lifting his hand for Chester to shake.

Running late, Lydia cursed the traffic as she pulled into the parking lot. Normally early, she was used to obtaining a spot close to the entrance but, today, no such luck. Glancing at her watch, she grabbed her purse and headed toward the front gate. Knowing she would be spending time with the journalists today already had her on edge.

The waving of signs caught her eye, and she sighed.

God, I wish they'd give that up. They've been doing that for ten years and you'd think, by now, they'd be sick of it. I know I am.

At least now, the protesters seemed to be calmer than they had been several years ago. When the NBAF first opened, she had been virtually attacked as she tried to walk into work. As she got closer, she glanced to the side, seeing Chester Thompson talking to a man in a suit. Wondering what that was about, it held her attention as she walked by.

Stunned, she recognized Eric from his profile. Smiling. Laughing. Shaking Chester's hand. Appearing for all the world to be his best bud. *Damn...and to think I slept with him.* If she was honest, she had done more than sleep with him. For two days he had filled her mind in a way that no other man had.

Glaring at the back of Eric's head, she marched up to the gate, swiped her badge over the reader, and stepped through with a nod toward the guard. Determined to put him out of her mind, she rushed through the halls to get to work.

Once inside the lab, she took a deep breath and closed her eyes, counting to ten.

"Hey, are you okay?" Jim asked.

She jerked her eyes open and plastered a smile on her face, "Yes, I'm fine. I just saw the protesters out front again this morning."

His brow furrowed, as he stated, "But they're out there a lot. At least they're better than they used to be. Did something happen this morning?"

Shaking her head, she said, "No. I guess it was just

me. I was running late, had to park in the very back of the parking lot, and for some reason seeing them this morning just put me on edge." Looking around, she asked, "Where's Beth?"

"She's already in the pen, getting ready for us." He moved over to the changing station and started shoving his feet into his boots.

Not wanting to hold him up, she tossed her purse and jacket on to her desk and hustled to do the same. By the time they finished with the morning exams, she knew she would have to forgo lunch in order to get her reports ready. Encouraging Jim and Beth to go eat, she sat at her desk, rubbing her forehead in an effort to still her headache. Her mind wandered back to Eric, and that thought only seemed to make her headache worse.

It's going to be a long day.

Once Eric had finalized his meeting with Chester, he made his way through the gate, registering as one of the visiting journalists. The guard at the door directed him, and the other journalists that were gathering around, to an auditorium. The visiting scientists had already had their introductory session and were being led into the research facilities.

Taking a seat, he looked around at the others. Not surprised, he viewed people of a variety of ethnicities, all wearing visitor press badges like himself. The thought ran through his mind that if he was able to obtain the badge, albeit through DHS, it would not be that hard for any terrorist group with some money and know-how to do the same.

"Hello."

Turning to the soft female voice coming from his left, he observed a petite, Asian woman smiling at him.

"Is this seat taken?" she asked.

Rising slightly, as his mother had always taught him, he smiled and said, "No. Please, help yourself." As she sat, he glanced at her badge, more interested in her representation than her name. Thailand.

"I'm so glad to be here," she remarked. "I fought for months with my agency to be able to represent them."

"Do you have a particular interest in this facility?" he asked.

Nodding, she said, "Absolutely. I was actually raised on a farm in China and know the devastation that animal diseases can cause. After I became a journalist, I traveled around, interviewing farmers and trying to get my foot in the door to talk directly to scientists. This will be a huge boost, not only to my career, but I'm hoping the work they do here will help us everywhere."

Before he had a chance to ask her more questions, the NBAF speakers came to the front of the room. After the initial introductions, a woman stepped forward to the microphone and introduced herself as Dr. Linda Hughley, the assistant director for NBAF and renowned expert on African Swine Fever. Medium height with dark hair pulled severely back from her face, she stared out over the group as she began to talk. For an hour, she lectured about the NBAF, how it came to be, the history of animal disease studies, and the importance of the work that they did at this facility.

Although he knew everything that was being said, he took notes just like the other journalists were doing. At the end of the session, they were told that they would hold off on questions until the final session several days hence.

Dr. Hughley explained, "I prefer to take questions from people who are knowledgeable about a subject. Until you have spent time at our facility and understand the scope of our work, I do not think that your questions would be appropriate."

A few of the journalists smiled, but he noticed some scowled at the implied insult.

Another assistant came to the podium, and said, "You already have the schedules that were emailed to you. You will need to be back here at the facility tomorrow morning to begin your tours and meet the veterinarian that will be taking over your information sessions." After wishing them to have a nice day, the meeting was adjourned.

Several of the journalists, including the young lady sitting next to him, were discussing where to go to have lunch. She turned and smiled up at him, and said, "Would you like to join us?"

While he should have been thrilled to take the opportunity to get to know some of them, he declined. "I'm afraid I already have plans for lunch. Perhaps maybe we can meet for dinner or drinks later?"

It appeared that quite a few the journalists were staying at the same hotel, one that was down the street from his. "I'll come this evening, and any of us who want to meet in the bar can do so. How would that be?"

Gaining the acquiescence of most, he smiled as they left the room. Turning back toward the podium, he noticed a silver-haired man walking toward him.

The man stopped directly in front of him, his gaze assessing, before lifting his hand. "Welcome to NBAF. Paul Royer."

Eric had been informed that Paul was to be his DHS liaison. Offering a firm handshake in return, he nodded. "Good to meet you, sir."

"Si Branson is an old friend of mine. I trust him explicitly, and he told me you're the man for the job. That's high praise."

"Glad to hear it. What have you got for me?"

Jerking his head back toward the podium, Paul said, "Besides this bullshit which anyone can get out of an Internet search, everyone's going to spend some time inside the facility. Obviously, no journalists will be going into the below-level research areas, but the bigwigs have decided that as much good press as they can get is not a bad thing. Considering that many of the journalists are representing countries that are currently facing an African Swine Fever epidemic, the idea is for them to take back the information to their countries, hoping for more international cooperation."

"And you've got some serious concerns about that or I wouldn't be here, right?"

"We've been getting threats from protesters since the idea was first conceived. The chatter is that some foreign money is coming into these groups, making them a real threat. As soon as I heard that Dr. Hughley was bringing in foreign journalists, I felt like it was too easy of a target for someone to slip in."

"And your biggest fear?"

"Honestly? North Korea. They would love to get a hold of some of our research. They're close to developing ways to take down other nations with biological warfare. So, you're going to be our eyes and ears with the journalists that are here. The doctor that you'll be with tomorrow has no idea of any of this. She's a veterinarian, not a researcher. She'll be explaining what we do here with the porcines and what type of research is going on. She'll be able to give the journalists plenty of information, without actually giving them anything concrete that someone either from North Korea, or someone who would pass information on to North Korea, could use."

Nodding, he indicated his understanding. "I'm gonna spend some time this evening with the journalists in an informal setting. I'll have one of my team do more digging on each one of them so that we'll know what we're dealing with. I'll also have an opportunity to see if I can find out if any of them has any tics to the protesting groups."

With a curt nod, Paul shook his hand again and escorted him out. A few minutes later, as he climbed into his car, he put Chester's address into his GPS.

So far, everything was going like clockwork.

7

Driving out of the small town of Manhattan, Eric admired the rolling hills of the surrounding prairie. Following his GPS, he made several turns on one country road after another until coming to the address Chester had given him.

Having investigated Chester before coming on this trip, he knew that he owned a sprawling ranch toward the Konza Prairie in the Flint Hills. As far as the eye could see, lush green hills and valleys spread out before him. Off in the distance, he could see the blackened, scorched earth where the prairie was being systematically burned off. He had read that usually controlled burning occurred in the late spring, but some ranchers would wait and burn in the fall.

At the end of the road leading to Chester's house, a long, red brick, one-story house came into view. Several outbuildings and a large barn sat further back from the house. Parking, he alighted from his car and walked to the front door.

Before he had a chance to knock, the door swung open and a short, stocky woman beamed up at him. "You must be Eric," she said, unlatching the screen door and pushing it open. "I'm Martha, Chester's wife. Come on in."

He stepped over the threshold and viewed a living room to the left. She invited him to follow her, and he walked down the hall toward the back of the house. Entering what was obviously the hub of the home, they made their way into a large, sunny kitchen connected to a dining room, containing a huge table in the middle. A den was also visible, with much more comfortable furnishings than he had seen in the living room.

"I was keeping my eye out because I figured a guest would use the front door," Martha said as she headed around the kitchen counter. "Folks around here always drive to the back and come in this door."

The door she indicated opened and Chester walked in, kicking his boots off by the door. Looking up, he smiled at Eric, and said, "Welcome. I see you met my Martha."

Martha looked over her shoulder, and said, "Go ahead and wash up, Chester. I'm serving up lunch right now."

Chester threw his hands up in the air and wiggled them back and forth, "Washed them in the workroom. Figured you'd have lunch ready and I didn't want to miss a bite."

He listened to the easy banter between Chester and

his wife and took the seat indicated to him. The door opened again, and he watched as a young couple, a woman that he had seen this morning outside of the NBAF, and another man that he had not met enter the house.

Chester introduced everyone, saying, "This is my daughter, Anne, and her husband, Terry. You may have met Eileen Jenkins this morning. She often meets us outside the gate. And this is her husband, Bertram. He's a lawyer and has helped us over the years to file various motions. I figured if you were good enough to want to do an interview, then I'd bring in more than just me for you to talk to."

Nodding, he replied, "This is wonderful, Chester. To have the opportunity to find out what's really going on is just what my boss at the news organization wants me to do."

Anne and Martha set platters on the table and his eyebrows lifted slightly at the amount of food. Roast beef, ham, green beans, corn, macaroni and cheese, salad, and large, fluffy rolls.

Martha cackled at his expression and said, "Chester and Terry work hard on the ranch, so I'm used to putting out a big spread at lunch. Plus, when he told me we were going to have a guest, I wanted to make sure we showed you some good, Midwestern hospitality."

Taking a cue from his hosts, he did not ask any questions during the meal. Martha's cooking was excellent, just as Chester had predicted, and he thanked her when the meal finished.

She waved his praise away, and said, "Go on into the den and I'll bring coffee in a few minutes."

Following the others, he sat in one of the chairs in the large, sunshine filled room. Chester sat in an easy chair that appeared to be molded to his body, and he assumed that was where many evenings were spent. Eileen and Bertram took two of the other chairs, and Terry sat on one end of the sofa. A moment later, Anne and Martha brought in a tray filled with coffee mugs and set it on the coffee table. Once served, they sat on the sofa as well.

Adopting the expression of the earnest journalist, he brought out his small recorder. "Do you have a problem with me recording this interview?"

Chester shook his head. "Hell, no. Can't say that there's anything new I'm going to tell you that I haven't been preaching for almost 15 years, so go ahead and record away."

"I was at the NBAF this morning, and heard their introductory speech—"

"Hmph, propaganda, you mean," Eileen groused.

"Eileen, hush," Martha chided. "We invited this man into our home, and we're going to listen to him and answer his questions." Turning back to him, she smiled and nodded, indicating for him to continue.

"Well," he cleared his throat, then continued, "this facility has been a long time coming. Have you been involved in voicing your protests for that long?"

The others turned to Chester, obviously giving him a chance to answer the question. Leaning back in his comfortable chair, Chester rested his hands over his stomach and began what appeared to him to be a practiced speech.

"When the government first wanted to find a location to replace the outdated Plum Island Facility, way back under George Bush's presidency, they eventually came up with six places. It took them two years to whittle down their choices from twenty-nine possible sites in 2006 to finally narrowing it down to six in 2008. Georgia, Mississippi, New York, North Carolina, Texas, and here in Kansas. As you can imagine, groups in all six places formed to oppose the facility. There were grassroot oppositions, as well as the National Grange, who spoke out against the idea. It was all for naught, because in 2008, Kansas was chosen as the site. I figure the other five places must've been jumping for joy in celebration, but I can tell you, here, we were getting ready to dig in for a war."

Not hearing anything he did not already know, he nonetheless nodded, somewhat enthusiastically, for Chester to continue. "I understand that some protesters are unhappy with the research that obviously takes place with some animals. Is this one of the points that you protest against?"

Shaking his head, Chester replied vehemently, "No, sir. Look out there at my pastures," and he swung his arm out to point beyond the window where the cattle were grazing in a field. "I'm not raising cattle for pets. I know that the animals I raise are going to be used for food. This is a way of life for us. The average American goes to the grocery store and buys their meat without giving a second thought as to where it came from. They slap it on the grill and enjoy eating, not once thinking about what they're putting in their mouth. And that's fine, I don't have a problem with that. And, research on animals and animal diseases is what keeps that meat on their plate safe for them to eat. That makes some people squeamish, but unless they're going to stop eating meat, then they need to realize that's just how the agricultural industry works."

"So, what are your reasons for not wanting it here?"

"Hell, man," Chester sputtered. "Why do you think they built the first facility out there on Plum Island, stuck in the Atlantic Ocean, back in the 1950s? The government put it out there because in the case of an accident, releasing the diseases they were studying, they wouldn't be hitting us right here in the middle of America. When that place got too old to be fixed up anymore, that's when they decided to look at places stateside. And I'll be goddamned if they didn't decide to stick it right in the middle of Kansas. Here! This part of the country is one of the major cattle and agricultural states. Any of that shit gets out of that building, and it would be worse than them dropping a hydrogen bomb on top of our heads!"

Chester's demeanor had devolved from a hospitable host to a man whose face was red with anger and whose chest heaved with righteous indignation. Eric watched the transformation occur before his eyes, wondering what the man was capable of in order to stop something he believed was a threat.

"So, you've been protesting since about 2006? That seems like an expensive endeavor."

Chester chuckled, the rumble deep in his chest. "You want to talk about expensive? That facility costs US taxpayers over a billion dollars. But don't worry over how much we've spent. We don't fight this battle alone. You'd be surprised how much support we have. Lotta people are fighting this battle with us, even if they're in the background. That's fine with me. I don't mind being the front-runner, as long as their pockets are deep."

"To be protesting something for over ten years seems like an exceptionally long time, considering that the construction of the facility moved forward, and the building is now functioning."

Chester leaned forward, his forearms resting on his knees as he clenched his fingers together. Pinning him with a hard stare, he replied, "We're not the only ones who want this thing shut down. When there's a war, you don't give up the fight. When an enemy is in your backyard, threatening everything you hold dear, you don't give up and you don't give in, even if you have to make a pact with the Devil."

Eric continued to ask questions for several more minutes, his understanding of Chester deepening as he came to terms with just what lengths the man would go to to protect the livelihood he perceived to be threatened.

That night, Eric sat at the bar in the hotel where many of the other press were staying. It was not as noisy as the bar from the night he met Lydia, being farther away from the college campus, but the comparison alone had him thinking back to meeting her. The time they spent together and his surprise when he woke up the next morning, discovering she had pulled a disappearing act, was hard to forget.

He knew he should have been grateful that she understood the parameters of their time spent together, but he could not help but be irritated that they had not had a chance to enjoy each other's company again before going their own separate ways. It had been a while since he had been with someone that he desired to spend more time with, and it was just his luck that it would happen somewhere far away from his home.

Hearing the noise of more people coming into the room pulled his attention away from his musings. He adjusted his glasses, making sure to casually look about the room so that the video transmitted to Chris would be comprehensive.

Seeing a few of the other journalists that he had met that morning, he lifted his hand and waved, watching as they came over and joined him at the large table. Introductions were made, and he discovered there were several people from China, South Korea, Russia, Georgia, Lithuania, Ukraine, and Africa in attendance. Listening to them chat, he learned that there were many others representing countries that were threatened with the African Swine Fever there for the conference as well.

"We didn't have much time to be introduced this morning," the pretty Thai journalist sitting next to him said. "I'm Anong Anuwat."

Eric introduced himself and then listened as the others around the table gave their names. Sitting across from him were a male and female, their eyes darting around the table and their lips slightly pinched. Looking at their name tags, he noted they were both from China. He held his gaze on them a moment longer to ensure Chris saw their names clearly. As he scanned everyone else's tags, he realized that the people seated closest to them represented South Korea and Russia, along with Thailand, and he wondered if the apparent animosity from the Chinese journalists was nationalistic, instead of personal.

A man sat down on his other side and immediately stuck his hand out. "I'm Bashiir…Bashiir Farah," he said, his white smile beaming. "I'm from Somalia, and this is my first time in the United States." After shaking his hand, he looked past him and smiled at Anong.

She reached across and shook Bashiir's extended hand as well, laughing, "I was in California last year at a media convention, but I didn't get to go anywhere other than Los Angeles. Being in the middle of the United States is such a thrill."

"Eric, do you live near here?"

He looked at the journalist from Russia, an older man with salt-and-pepper hair. "No, I live on the East Coast," he replied, keeping his answer vague.

"I find the geography of the United States so confusing," Seo-yun Park, the female South Korean journalist, said. "I traveled some in Asia but find that Americans are much less diverse."

Uncertain what she meant, he was about to ask,

when her male partner, Ji-Ho, explained, "You have one language here, as opposed to each Asian country."

Normally, Eric hated small talk but forced himself to participate in the conversations while simultaneously assessing the other journalists. Though they talked with ease when directly addressed, he noted with interest, the segregation amongst them. The two from South Korea talked easily with he and Anong but limited their conversation with others. Bashiir had no difficulty speaking to any of them and seemed quite keen on learning everything he could. The two journalists from China, Wang Xiu and Zhang Wei, appeared to view everyone at the table with suspicion, and Egor, from Russia, kept mostly to himself.

Seeing some of the other journalists come into the bar, he excused himself and made the rounds, making introductions and inserting himself in their conversations. After several hours of this, he said his goodbyes and headed back to his hotel.

Thinking of his previous evening with Lydia, he could not help but feel this evening paled greatly in comparison.

8

Entering his room, Eric was ready to collapse on his bed when he saw Chris sitting on the sofa, literally bouncing with excitement. Shutting the door, he pulled off his press badge and glasses and walked over to the chair. Plopping down, he loosened his tie and leaned back.

"That was fuckin' amazing," Chris said, his voice as animated as his body. "The way you worked that room...the way you were able to get people to start talking...the way you were able to keep the camera on the various people around."

Lifting his head, his expression one of utter boredom, he said, "Please tell me you were able to get something from all of that."

"Yes!"

Chris started typing on his laptop, his knee bouncing up and down. Eric leaned his head back again, assuming Chris would let him know what he found as soon as he was ready.

"Okay, take a look at this," Chris said, turning his laptop around and jumping up from the sofa to kneel on the floor so that they were both facing the screen. "Of the two journalists from South Korea, only one of them was actually born and raised there." He pointed to a photograph of Ji-Ho Kim, and said, "He is originally from China, near the port city of Dandong. That's an easy connection between China and North Korea."

"How long has he been a journalist for South Korea?"

"That's the interesting part. I can't find any information that he's ever been a journalist, anywhere, much less for South Korea."

"What about Seo-yun Park? Any information on her? I wonder if she knows about Ji-Ho."

"I've been able to verify the government-run publication she works for, so she's legit, but I don't know if she's aware that Ji-Ho's not who he says he is. If they've never worked together before, it's possible this is her first time meeting him as well. But, I'll keep looking."

Sucking in a breath, Eric said, "Okay, so he goes on our suspicious list, along with Chester. What else did you get from tonight's agonizing small-talk fest that I had to engage in?"

Chris cackled out loud, slapping his knee. "Can't believe you don't get a rush from being out in the middle of everything, digging out information, and figuring out who we're up against."

Pinching the bridge of his nose with his forefinger

and thumb, he shook his head slowly. "I'm more of an action man. I wondered when I was tasked for this job if I was the right person, considering I hate having to spend a lot of time around a ton of people."

Chris continued clicking on his laptop, and said, "The two journalists from China check out, both their names and the news organizations they represent. Zhang and Wang…" Chuckling, he said, "Didn't you have a hard time keeping a straight face when they introduced themselves?"

"Jesus, Chris. If you ever expect to get out in the field, you'd better have some more cultural sensitivity training."

"I'm not culturally insensitive," Chris said, his brow lowering. "I just think it's funny that their names rhyme. I'd feel the same if we were named Stan and Dan…or Fred and Ted…or Bob and—"

"I get it." Wanting Chris to finish his information, he said, "Keep going. What else have you got?"

"The Russian guy, Egor, seems to check out as well." Sniggering, Chris looked up and mumbled, "Sorry. Just made me think of Frankenstein's Igor." Clearing his throat, he continued, "Bashiir from Somalia also checks out." Wiggling his eyebrows, he said, "And, that cute girl from Thailand also checks out. Man, you sure are lucky. The way she was looking at you, all you had to do was crook your finger and I think she would have followed you anywhere."

Torn between wanting to thank Chris for his quick investigative skills and wanting to kick him out for his dumbass comments, he sighed. "Okay, Chris. That's the first group of people I met. I need you to keep doing the same thing on the rest of the group. We need to know if there's anyone who is not who they say they are, does not work for who they say they work for, and especially if they have any monetary ties to one of the protesting groups."

Standing, Chris grabbed his laptop and nodded. "No problem, boss. I've got secured lines and have already sent my info back to DHS headquarters so they can help search through all this information. If there are links, we'll find them."

Closing the door behind Chris, he rolled his shoulders and moved his neck back and forth, hearing it crack. Having grown used to his more solitary lifestyle in Vermont, he found spending the day with large groups of people to be exhausting.

Double checking the security of his room, he headed into the bathroom, stripped and stepped into the shower. While he tried to relax his body with the warm water pelting his skin, his mind was unable to stop processing the day's information.

If Ji-Ho Kim is actually from China, why is he masquerading as a journalist from South Korea? Where does he currently live? And for how long? Who was Chester alluding to when he talked about the deep pockets of those who would like to stop the NBAF?

After he stepped out of the shower and toweled off, he pulled on his boxers and brushed his teeth. Flipping off the light, he slid under the covers and lay back on the bed with his arms behind his head.

And the biggest question of them all? I wonder what Lydia is doing tonight?

Rolling over, he punched the pillow, willing sleep to come.

Lydia glanced at the clock on the wall the next morning, wondering if Beth was just late. Her phone rang and, picking it up, she heard the unhappy voice of her coworker.

"I'm so sorry, but I've got to take my dog into the clinic over on campus today. Crazy thing got in the garbage and ate something he shouldn't have. I'll try to be in later this afternoon if possible."

Assuring Beth that it was no problem, her thoughts went in the opposite direction. With only two of them it would take longer to do the checks on the swine, and she was expecting the assigned journalists to show up sometime that morning. Turning to Jim, she said, "Looks like we're on our own today. I guess we'd better get started."

After getting into their boots and gloves, the two went into the pen where the pigs were kept. Kneeling, she grabbed a pig, checked its ear for the tag, called it out, and then she and Jim together examined the animal. As she scooted over to the next one, he entered the information into his tablet.

They were only halfway through, when Jim was called away by their supervisor. Shooting her an apologetic look, he left the pen and headed out of the animal area. Frustrated, she stood with her hands on her hips, as the pigs rooted around her feet.

Eric and the other journalists filed out of the conference room and stood in line to begin the next portion of the seminar. Now knowing that Ji-Ho was not who he said he was, he watched the young man carefully to see if he formed any alliances or gave off any information. The camaraderie between Ji-Ho and Seo-yun appeared genuine, but he was determined to get her alone sometime to ask how long she had known the man.

"You will be paired with Dr. Hughes, one of our porcine veterinarians." The NBAF employee making the announcement glanced to the side as a man walked up. "Oh, Jim, here are your charges."

He watched as the tall, dark-haired veterinarian walked forward, an easy manner about him. Calling for the group to follow him, the affable young man turned and led them down the hall he had come from.

"Nice to meet you, Dr. Hughes," Eric said, as they fell in step, the other journalists right behind.

"Oh, I'm not Dr. Hughes. I'm Jim, Dr. Hughes' intern. I was called to escort you to our work area. We are down a person today, so Dr. Hughes is incredibly busy." As though concerned his words had sounded unfriendly, Jim rushed to add, "You're really lucky to have the chance to meet her. She's an excellent veterinarian and dedicated this organization. She's very knowledgeable about porcine."

"Young and fresh out of veterinary medical school?" Egor asked, an edge to his harsh voice.

Eric caught the disdain in Egor's question and glanced to the side to see what Jim's response would be.

Jim's eyes narrowed, as he replied, "Dr. Hughes is not fresh out of veterinary school. She practiced in the field for a number of years before joining the NBAF."

As they walked down the hall, Jim's voice lowered just for Eric's ears. "If he acts like a jackass around her, I might be tempted to take him out behind the woodshed."

Eric held back his grin, but admired Jim's loyalty. "Have you worked with her long?"

"No, she came on board when the facility opened, and I've only been her intern for about two months. I wasn't kidding when I said she was a good veterinarian, but she's also just a really nice person. She was widowed years ago and raised her daughter, who's now in college, on her own, all while finishing her degrees. She's one of those people who can handle whatever is thrown at her. We were just told a couple of days ago that she would be working with you guys, but she jumped in, ready to do her part."

They moved through several sets of doors, down long halls twisting and turning as they approached the back side of the facility. Jim raised his voice to address the whole group as he said, "We have a number of veterinarians on staff to take care of the animals that we have here. It's my understanding that your focus on our facility is specifically dealing with the outbreak of African Swine Fever. You'll be spending the next day with the pigs." With that introduction, Jim pushed through the next set of doors and the group walked in.

Finding himself standing in a large room housing multiple pens, Eric jolted at the sudden cacophony of pigs grunting and squealing, as well as the odor of straw, dirt, feed, and only a hint of fecal matter. A woman wearing navy scrubs, with her feet jammed in muddy, rubber boots, was standing with her back to them, a hose in her hand as she filled a water trough.

Eric was further shocked at the size of the pigs in the pen that she was in. *Jesus, I thought they were little piglets.* A large pig bumped into the woman, and her feet slipped on the wet floor. Too far away to assist, he watched as she fell to her ass. Scrambling, she jumped up, planted her hands on her now wet hips. Looking down, she fussed at the pig.

"Dr. Hughes!" Jim yelled.

The woman looked up, and he was surprised yet again, even more so than from the sound and the smells in the room. The woman whose ass was now covered in wet mud, was none other than his Lydia. The instant her gaze landed on him, her smile dropped from her face, and her eyes widened in shock. He started to smile, but her eyes quickly narrowed, and she glared.

What the fuck?

9

Lydia recovered quickly from her shock at seeing Eric with his press badge clipped to his front pocket and surrounded by the other journalists. In an attempt to ignore the heat flooding her face, she forced a smile upon her lips. She was aware of the state of her muddy clothing and equally aware of having landed on her ass in front of everyone. Seeing the journalists staring back at her, she wondered if any of them had ever been in a pigpen.

Keeping her eyes pointedly away from Eric, she walked over and nodded her greeting. "Good morning," she said. Holding up her soiled gloved hands, she joked, "I'll wait for proper introductions when I can shake your hands."

The laughter of some met her ears, but she was also very aware that some of the journalists stared at her, unsmiling. She glanced toward Jim, who lifted his shoulders in a slight shrug, as though he was not sure what to do.

Deciding to jump right in, she said, "I'm Dr. Lydia Hughes, one of the veterinarians here. I practiced with my own large animal clinic before doing a porcine research internship here at the Kansas Veterinary Medicine School. After my internship, the NBAF was nearing completion and I began work here shortly thereafter. Over the next few days, you will become acquainted with the scope of the porcine research done here, while your scientist counterparts will be with the researchers learning about specific techniques and methods. I know you've already heard about how necessary the work here is for the safety of our food sources, both biological and agricultural."

Unable to help herself, her gaze slid to the side, searching out Eric. His dark eyes were staring straight at her, and even given her cool reception of him, it was not hard to see warmth coming from them. She had seen those eyes from only a few inches away as his body rocked into hers. She felt the heat of blush hit her face once more, only this time she knew it was from memories of the night they had spent together.

Blinking, she noticed as his lips curved into a slight smile, as though he knew exactly what she was thinking about. Irritated that she was letting those memories overshadow the fact that she had seen him happily conversing with one of the protesters, she blinked again, this time to refocus on the group.

Clearing her throat, she continued, "Twice a day, my coworkers and I are in charge of assessing each of the pigs in this large room." Sweeping her hand out toward the other pens, she added, "They are divided by age and one of our tasks is to assure their health.

"Of course, we realize there are groups that protest what is done here, but the work and research from this facility goes into ensuring that the food on the plates of not only Americans, but of everyone around the world, is safe. I know that many of you represent countries that are hoping to emulate the work that we do here."

Avoiding Eric's eyes, she finished, "If you will please follow Jim, he will take you into the next room and show you the basic layout of our office. That will give me the opportunity to clean up so that I may be more presentable."

This time more smiles met her, plus some bows as the journalists obediently turned and began to follow Jim. She looked around, her eyes scanning over the pigs that she had just been dealing with and spotted the one she wanted to have words with.

Stomping over, she looked down and grumbled, "Thanks a lot. Bumping into me right when everyone was coming into the room. Did you do that on purpose?"

The large pig raised its head up and looked at her while still crunching its food. She leaned over and rubbed her hand over its back before scratching behind its ears. "I still think you're a miscreant and did that on purpose!"

Grunting was the only response the pig gave her before turning back down to its food. Shaking her head, she turned to walk out of the pen. Her feet stumbled as she saw Eric still standing there, a wide smile on his face.

Lips tight, she cocked her head to the side. "I think the instructions were for you to follow Jim along with the others."

His eyes stayed on her as she made it to the pen gate, moved through, and turned to assure that it was locked behind her. She wanted to pretend that it did not matter, but she hated that her hair was falling out of its ponytail, her ass and boots were covered in muck and, seeing his eyes drop to her cheek quickly before he grinned, she was fairly sure that she had a smudge.

Moving past him, he halted her with a single word said in his rich, deep voice. "Lydia."

His voice had the same effect as the first time he had said her name and, she had to admit, she loved the sound of it on his lips. Steeling her spine, she turned to the side and looked at him. "Eric."

He stared at her for a moment, as though trying to figure her out. Deciding not to give him any more time, she said, "If you'll excuse me, I need to get back to the group."

His eyes lazily moved from her face, down her body, to her muck-covered boots, before dragging back up again. His lips curved slightly as he said, "It's good to see you again. And, I confess, interesting to see you here."

Narrowing her eyes as she turned her body to face him fully, she asked, "What do you mean? You don't think a woman can be a veterinarian or researcher?"

"No, that's not it," he explained, his smile now

widening over his face. "I just didn't imagine you cavorting with pigs."

Sucking in a quick breath, she leaned forward, and said, "For your information, pigs are highly intelligent, more so than dogs. They are very social and make friends easily. And on top of that, they're loyal." Turning, she walked away from him, heading to an employee locker room, knowing she needed a quick shower and change of clothing before joining the group again. The back of her neck burned, and she knew it was due to his gaze staying on her. Knowing that her ass was covered in muck only served to bring the heat of blush back to her face. Again.

Eric watched as Lydia headed out of the large animal area. Not even trying to keep the smile from his face, he admired the sway of her dirt-covered hips. Unable to remember the last time he was this attracted to a woman, his smile slowly drooped as he reflected on her obvious irritation with him.

We both knew that it was for one night only, although I wouldn't mind another night. But she's the one who slipped out of the hotel room the next morning.

With no time to discern the cause of her anger, he hustled back through the doors that Jim had taken the group through. The journalists were listening to Jim as he explained the computer system NBAF used in analyzing the healthy porcine bloodwork and other bodily systems. He had no interest in the topic, only studying the faces of

83

the journalists. He listened to their questions, but more importantly, watched their body language.

Bashiir, Anong, and Seo-yun appeared genuinely interested, their questions readily answered by Jim and, from his responses, they appeared to be relevant. Wang and Zhang stood over to the side, their eyes rarely on Jim, but often looking to each other as they took notes. Egor and Ji-Ho were standing next to each other, and he observed that they seemed to be avoiding eye contact.

Curious. Avoiding eye contact because they don't want to look at each other...or don't want to appear that they have any type of connection?

He heard a door open directly behind him, and the scent of antiseptic soap wafted by. He had taken the position near the door, hoping to be there as soon Lydia walked in. He was not disappointed as she stopped next to him.

Glancing to the side, he saw that she was wearing clean scrubs, rubber-soled clogs on her feet, and her hair was freshly brushed back into a neat ponytail. Her face now scrubbed clean, with just a hint of makeup, was as alluring as ever.

She continued to face forward toward the journalists and Jim, and he smiled at her obvious attempt to ignore him. The information that Jim had given him now came slamming back to the forefront of his mind. A widow. A single mom to a grown child. Staring at her, she did not appear to be over the age of forty. *She must've been a teenager when she gave birth.*

As though she could follow the thoughts moving through his head, she jerked her head around, her ponytail slapping her cheek with its force. Keeping her voice low, she growled, "Stop staring at me!"

His smile widened, and he said, "I can't help it. My eyes always go to the most beautiful thing in the room. And that, Lydia, is you."

Somehow, Lydia managed to get through the rest of the morning with Jim's help. The group was released to meet in the cafeteria for lunch, and she breathed a sigh of relief as the journalists filed out of the room. She had already told Jim to make sure he left for lunch, since he had worked so hard in Beth's absence.

She dropped her chin and stared at her shoes for a moment, relishing the quiet in the room. She had not realized how much she enjoyed her quiet work, spent mostly with Beth and Jim, only broken up occasionally with the staff meetings that she was required to attend. She even considered the pigs to be more peaceful than a group of journalists filled with questions and comments and never-ending discussions.

A hand landed on her shoulder, and she jumped. Whirling around, her wide eyes landed on Eric. "What on earth are you still doing here?"

His smile from earlier was gone, and he bit out, "You and me need to talk."

Huffing, she stepped back so that his hand was no

longer on her shoulder. "I cannot imagine what you and I have to talk about."

"That. That right there."

Her brow crinkled, and her head jerked back slightly. "What?"

His fists landed on his hips, his gaze pinning her to the spot. "I thought we had a good time together," he declared. "You were the one who left before I woke up. So, I want to know what's changed, and why you're so angry?"

Snorting in anger, she said, "I don't owe you any explanation."

She started to walk past him when his arm shot out, his hand clamping on her upper arm. The hold was firm but not painful. She looked down at his hand and then lifted her gaze to his. Opening her mouth, she did not get anything out before he continued.

"Lydia, I agree that just because my cock has been in you gives me no rights to an answer. But given the fact that when you came, you held my gaze and breathed my name, that tells me you were not just getting off, and I know I sure as hell wasn't. So, I'd like to know what happened between then and now."

She stood for a moment, her insides quivering, but it had nothing to do with anger and more to do with the fact that his hand on her arm sent tingles throughout her body. Hating that fact, she turned slowly to face him. Her voice now calm and steady, she replied, "While it would be unfair for me to consider the press to be my enemy, I saw you smiling and laughing with Chester Thompson, and believe me, he is the enemy."

The afternoon crawled as Eric and the journalists continued their tour of the porcine area and the basic research being accomplished. They were not allowed on the lower floors of the building, where the more dangerous research was going on. Every time he was near Lydia, his fingers twitched to pull her close. Just standing next to her, he fought the urge to grab her hand, drag her through one of the doors, press his body up against hers, and explain that he was not who she thought he was.

Clenching his jaw, he knew that line of thinking was fruitless. As far as she knew, he was a member of the press who was going to be talking to protesters as well as scientists and reporting back on whatever he learned. Unable to keep the heavy sigh from slipping through his lips, he caught her staring at him, her brow furrowed as though she were trying to figure him out. *At least that's better than her glaring and hating my guts.*

Looking away, he focused his attention back on the group of journalists. Seo-yun and Ji-Ho had been staying fairly close together since they had come back from lunch. Now, Egor had moved to where he was standing between Wang and Zhang.

It was second nature to not look at them as just part of the press, but as representatives of their various countries. Earlier, South Korea appeared close to Russia, and now Russia was right in the middle of China. Because they were unable to have any electronic devices inside the NBAF, they were each taking notes with pen and paper. He felt like a schoolteacher, staring at the pupils taking a test, when he caught Wang's gaze staying on the notebook in which Egor was writing.

Moving closer to the large computer screen that Lydia was referring to in her speech, he made the pretense of taking off his glasses in order to clean them, holding them up occasionally as though looking at the lens to determine there were no smudges. In doing so, he focused them over Egor's shoulder, making sure that Chris would be able to see the notes that were being written.

Egor glanced behind him and glared, but he lifted his shoulders in a shrug, and said, "Can't see a damn thing without my glasses."

Besides the camera in his glasses, Chris had fitted him with another one today, knowing there would be a lot of movement and people to keep up with. Chris had explained that the one now in his tie had a wide-angle lens that was able to see and record information at almost 180°. Taking advantage of that, he walked around the room slowly, taking notes as a journalist would, while keeping an eye on all the occupants. As Lydia finished her portion of the afternoon's lecture, Jim took over to complete the discussion and lead the group outside, so that she would be able to get back into the animal area.

As she walked past the group now exiting, he moved in the opposite direction and made his way toward her. Glaring at him, she whispered, "Have you got ants in your pants? You've done nothing but walk around for almost an hour!"

His lips curved as he responded, "Now, Lydia. You know what I have in my pants."

"Urgh," she growled, pushing past him to go back to the pens.

As she shoved through the doors, he could not help but chuckle. Her blush indicated she was not as unaffected as she pretended to be.

Sitting in the chair in his hotel room with his feet propped up on the coffee table, Eric listened as Chris excitedly explained what he was finding.

"Of course, I don't read Russian, but I'm sending this to the language guru at DHS that Silas put me in contact with. You got really good shots, but a few are kind of wiggly."

Having been staring at the ceiling for a few minutes, he dropped his chin and pinned Chris with a glare. "I did the best I could considering I could hardly walk up to Egor and say, 'Pardon me, would you please let me get a clear picture of your notes, which coincidentally the Chinese journalist is already staring at."

Chris cackled, and said, "You're so funny!", before staring back at his computer screen.

Eric dropped his head back and continued staring at the ceiling, thinking the last thing he wanted to do was provide Chris with any comedic relief. "Once you get finished going through some of what we got today, see if anyone has a tie to the Foundation for Liberating Animals. That's who I'm interviewing tomorrow, and I'd like to know if any of the journalists here have been involved with them."

Chris nodded and, with a few more clicks on his computer, said, "I know you've already done your research on them, but you need to be really careful. These people are not just animal-rights activists, they're extremists. They consider themselves to be above the law when it comes to interrupting scientific research, and that includes death threats, violence, arson, vandalism...hell, the list goes on and on."

Shaking his head, he thought about the difference between the FLA and Chester's ideals. According to Chester, he had no problem with research, being involved in the animal industry himself. Chester just hated the risk of contamination of his land and cattle. But, he reminded himself, that did not mean that Chester was not involved in threats to the facility.

Chris continued to search but so far was unable to come up with an overt connection between any of the journalists and either of the protesting groups. Just as he was about to close up his computer and head back to his room, Eric stopped him with a request.

"Don't read anything into this, but can you get me the home address for Dr. Lydia Hughes?"

Chris' blue eyes widened for a few seconds before grinning widely. Much to Eric's satisfaction, Chris made no comment, other than, "No problem, man." After only a few clicks on his keyboard, he said, "Just sent it to your email. That way, when you open it on your phone, it can go straight to your GPS." Closing the top of his computer, he nodded his head as he stood and walked out of his room, calling out, "See you tomorrow."

Eric continued sitting in the chair for a few more minutes, his mind filled with various aspects of this mission. He had no idea at this moment if he was getting any closer to finding out the information that Silas wanted. Hearing his phone ding with the incoming email containing Lydia's address, all other thoughts left his mind, and a satisfied smile curved his lips.

This was not what Eric had expected, nor what he liked. While his visit with Chester had been friendly, his interview with the FLA had so far rivaled his most serious cloak and dagger missions.

He was picked up in front of his hotel by a taxi driver whose instructions were to take him to a particular bar just outside of town. Left out front, he waited as per the instructions, then another person picked him up in a dark SUV with tinted windows. Climbing into the back seat, he was instructed to place a blindfold over his eyes.

The drive took almost fifteen minutes before the SUV came to a stop, and he was told to stay put. He could hear the driver alight from the vehicle and the sounds of footsteps as they walked around to his door. Once his door opened, a firm, but not painful, hand on his arm guided him out. With the barest amount of light from the bottom of the blindfold, he could see that he was walking on asphalt.

Moving through a door, he continued down a tiled floor. The blindfold was taken off after he entered a room, and he found himself in a comfortable office. A door opened and, much to his surprise, a man walked in wearing a mask, the type found in a Halloween store.

"Good afternoon," the man said, chuckling as he spread his hands out to the side. "I realize all of this subterfuge appears to be over the top, but our work is so important and there are those who find our methods unacceptable."

Surprised that the man used a digital voice changer as well, Eric asked, "Unacceptable or illegal?"

"Both, I should say." The man sat down behind a small desk, and said, "I know you represent a scientific press, so I find it interesting that you want an interview with the Foundation for Liberating Animals."

"I'm trying to gain a deeper understanding of the NBAF, and to do so it also behooves me to understand those who are against it. I have spoken with Chester Thompson—"

The man made a rude noise, biting out, "A ridiculous and feckless exercise on Mr. Thompson's part."

Lifting his eyebrows, Eric said, "Before you begin your explanation of your organization, perhaps you would be good enough to give me your name."

"John Doe. After we speak today, you'll understand why I use the name. My work is important, but as I said earlier, I don't feel bound by society's laws."

Nodding slowly, he said, "Okay, so tell me why your work is important. Let's start with that. I've read that you have no problem with the theft of animals, vandalism, coercion, and other methods to, in your words, liberate animals from researchers."

"Yes, we believe in direct action in pursuit of animal-rights and will take any method necessary to free animals where we can."

"It's also said that you're considered to be terrorists."

"We desire to overshadow any debate on the need for using animals in any type of research. It may be as simple as creating fear so that a scientist will stay silent and, doing so, will help to turn public opinion against the research."

"So, are you admitting that you consider yourself to be a terrorist?"

"If by terrorist you mean do we invoke terror? Then yes, I believe the word terrorist could apply. Although, we prefer animal activist."

"How organized is your organization?"

"I can tell you that we are active in over forty countries, but if you're asking if we have an email list and newsletter, the answer is no," John Doe chuckled. "We go to great lengths to cover our tracks."

"What do you want my readers to take away from this article?" Eric knew he was playing a part but found himself truly wanting to know the answer to this question.

John Doe was quiet for just a moment, then sighed heavily. "We are the ones who are considered to be terrorists at worst, criminals at best, but all we strive to do is save the innocent."

"With new laws in place for research facilities, do you still feel relevant?"

"Man has a great capacity for cruelty," John Doe said. "We will always be relevant."

Eric countered, "Surely you do not think cruelty applies solely to acts against animals. After all, your organization has been linked to attacking people, fire-bombs, blowing up buildings—"

"In the pursuit of what is right, there will always be casualties," John Doe stated, his voice harsh.

"So, it is fine to harm humans, just not animals?"

The room was silent, no answer forthcoming.

Changing the direction in the interview, Eric asked, "With your group being so international, do you get money from other governments?"

John Doe sat very still for a long moment and Eric did not think he was going to answer the question. Finally, John said, "We get donations from a variety of sources and do not turn down any assistance in the pursuit of our cause."

As the interview came to a close, he was taken back to his hotel the same way in which he was brought. Bypassing Chris' room, he walked directly to his, finding his thoughts tangled in his mind. Moving directly into the shower, he stood under the hot spray of water. With his hands pressed flat against the tile, he allowed the water to pelt his back.

Having dealt with other types of terrorists when he was a SEAL in Afghanistan, he knew that to terrorists, their cause was right and just, regardless of their methods. Both John Doe and Chester Thompson admitted to not turning down money that was offered to further their cause.

Climbing out of the shower, he toweled off and pulled on fresh clothes. Hearing a knock on his door, he opened it to Chris, and said, "Keep digging on the money trail from the FLA and Chester's group. While Chester, at least, sounds like a sane man, I can tell you the FLA will stop at nothing to try to shut down the facility here. And keep digging to see what link we can find between any of our journalists and groups that may be paying the protesters money."

"Sure, boss," Chris said.

He shoved his feet into his boots, his wallet into his back pocket, and grabbed his leather jacket. "I'm heading out."

"Going to find that pretty vet you were asking me about?"

Shooting a look over his shoulder at Chris, he grinned but did not reply.

Lydia stood with one hand on the refrigerator door and stared at the contents, wishing something would jump out and fix itself for dinner. It was not that she did not have food to cook, but after the last several days, the desire to cook for just herself no longer held any interest.

If she were honest, it had been hard to think of cooking for just one since Caroline had left for college. Empty nest was real, and it was a bitch.

She considered calling her, then looked at the clock on the stove. *No, Caroline is probably at dinner with friends. Or studying. Or on a date.* That last thought gave her pause as she thought back to when she was Caroline's age and already pregnant. While she was never sorry that she had her, she truly hoped her daughter was better with birth control, wanting Caroline to finish college first.

She was still standing with the refrigerator door

open, when she heard a knock on the front door. Not expecting anyone, she moved through the short hall and opened the door. Stunned, she observed Eric standing on her front porch. Her heart skipped a beat at the sight of him, but she pushed that feeling to the side, drawing upon her irritation at him.

"What are you doing here?"

He opened his mouth to answer, but she spoke before he had a chance.

"And how did you know where I lived?"

Once more, he opened his mouth, but was unable to speak.

"Wait," she bit out, throwing her hand up. "I don't even want to know. I don't even care. As far as I'm concerned, you can turn around and leave."

"I just wanted to see you."

His simple words had the effect of dousing her fiery thoughts with water. She had only spent one night with him, but his face was as familiar to her as someone she had known for years. The intensity of his blue-green eyes staring back at her, and she faltered in her resolve to kick him out before he ever came in.

As she silently considered her options, he continued to stand on her front stoop with his hands shoved in his jean pockets which, she had to admit, fit him exceptionally well and had her heart skipping a beat at the memory of him out of his jeans. His dark shirt was tight across his chest, and she sucked in a breath, feeling the lack of oxygen to her brain. Lifting her gaze back to his face, the vulnerability she witnessed made her want to wipe away his uncertainty.

She sighed, the desire to spend more time with him winning out over the desire to send him on his way. Stepping back, she opened the door wider and waved her hand to the side. "Okay, Eric, you can come in."

A smile crossed his face, and her heart skipped again. A sudden thought popped into her head, and as he entered her house, her hand moved up quickly, her palm on his chest, halting his progress. "Wait." Her eyes narrowed, and her gaze hardened. "Is this a social visit or are you wearing your journalist hat right now?"

"There is nothing journalistic about my visit," he promised, his gaze holding hers. "This is all personal. You want the truth? Here it is. We had a night that meant something to me. I know we said it wouldn't go beyond the night, but it was special. I just wanted to see you again. I can't stand the idea that we parted the way we did. Talking with Chester, I was just doing my job. I'm not out to hurt you, Lydia. Not in any way."

Her heartbeat rushed as she heard the sincerity in his voice and read the intense look on his face. Her breath left her lungs slowly, and she nodded. No longer able to pretend differently, she said, "Yeah...I know. I felt the same."

His face broke into a wide smile as he continued into her home, hesitating in the small vestibule.

"Do you want something to eat? Or maybe something to drink?" she asked.

He opened his mouth and then snapped it shut quickly again, as though uncertain how he should answer.

A giggle slipped out, and she said, "This isn't a test, Eric, I promise. There is no wrong answer."

His smile replaced his uncertainty, and he replied, "Then, if you're having something, I will too."

"I was actually in the process of staring into my refrigerator hoping that the chef genie would appear and make something out of whatever the food genie had magically left in there."

Barking out a laugh, he said, "Well, why don't we take a look together and see what we can find."

Not having a reason to deny his suggestion, she nodded silently and turned to walk into the kitchen. Once there, she reopened the refrigerator door and stepped back. Throwing her hands out to the side in her best game show hostess pose, she quipped, "Make yourself at home. If you can fulfill the role of either food or chef genie, I'll be grateful."

Eric stepped forward and bent, peering into the refrigerator. Straightening, he also opened her freezer door. Turning suddenly, he said, "Why don't you have a seat, and let me take care of this. You've been working hard with all of us around and were down an assistant, so I know you're tired."

Lydia stared at him for a few beats but, once more, only saw sincerity on his face. Refusing to spend any time trying to analyze his motives, she focused on his words and knew he was right. She was tired. Nodding, she offered a small smile, and said, "I'll take you up on that offer."

Instead of leaving the kitchen, she sat at the kitchen counter on one of the two stools. He did not seem to need her assistance, so she remained quiet, at first trying to avoid looking at him and then finally giving in to the desire and watching.

As Eric bustled around her kitchen, she saw that his gaze drifted over to her as well. After he buttered a large frying pan, he took out some of the deli ham, the half onion that was wrapped in plastic wrap, and a bag of frozen peas from the fridge and freezer. Nuking some of the peas, he chopped the ham and onion. Opening her refrigerator once more, he grabbed four eggs and a block of cheddar cheese that she was sure had mold on one side.

"I don't want you to think that I'm a terrible cook," Lydia said, surprised that she did not want him to think poorly of her. "My life situation has changed recently, and I find cooking to no longer be something that I enjoy as much."

He looked over his shoulder as he scrambled eggs and offered a smile. After trimming the mold, he grated some of the cheese. Within a few minutes, he was plating an omelet split in half between them. The scent was delicious, and her mouth watered.

Jumping up, she opened the refrigerator and said, "I'm not sure what you want to drink. I don't think beer or wine would go with this."

He lifted an eyebrow as the corner of his lips twitched. "Is that milk still good?"

"Yes. I tend to be a big cereal eater, so I buy milk often."

"Then milk it is," he said. "In fact, milk will be perfect."

They sat down at the small table tucked in the eating nook of the kitchen. Taking her first bite, Lydia closed her eyes and moaned. "This is so good." Opening her eyes, she stared directly at him. "It's exactly what I needed. Thank you."

He shook his head. "You don't have to thank me, Lydia. I understand why you were upset with me and I just couldn't walk away with you thinking the worst of me."

She swallowed her bite, then shook her head. "I was sitting here watching you cook and thinking about my actions. I'm the one who owes you an apology, Eric." She saw him about to protest, and said, "No. Please, let me finish."

He inclined his head slightly, and she continued. "When I was in vet med school, I was not sure which specialty I wanted to pursue. I considered small animal, but to be honest, I didn't want to spend my days seeing one cat or dog right after the other. I was never a horse person, although I like horses. But," she grinned and shrugged, "most veterinarians who specialize in equine have been around horses most of their lives." She chuckled slightly, and added, "The rest of us consider equine veterinarians to be a little...uh...different. Horse people are just all about the horse."

Lydia took several more bites, the warm food settling her stomach and easing her tension. The mood in the kitchen was calm and, just like when she had first met Eric, his attention was riveted on her.

"I had friends that were more into research or government veterinary medicine and planned on doing their internships in that. Neither of those options appealed to me, and I needed to get finished so that my financial obligation was over, and I could start making money. I discovered that I enjoyed the outdoors, working with farmers, and cattle, sheep, goats, and pigs were great to work with. So, I decided that large animal veterinary medicine was for me. After working for several years, I wanted to do an internship here at KSU's vet med school."

She looked down at their empty plates and leaned back in her chair, "Oh my goodness, I'm just talking about myself but haven't gotten around to my apology."

"That's okay," Eric said, leaning back as well. "I love hearing you talk about your work." He stood and collected the plates, and she jumped up to assist.

"Here, let me," she insisted, and took the plates from him. Rinsing them off she placed them in the dishwasher as he rinsed out the pan. Uncertain as to what he wanted to do, she hesitated as she dried her hands on the dish towel.

"Why don't we sit some more, and you can keep telling me about your work," he suggested.

Agreeing, Lydia led him into the living room, and he settled on the sofa while she plopped into her comfortable chair.

"Anyway, the point I was eventually getting to, is that no matter what area of veterinary medicine you specialize in, research is a huge part of what we do. Animals are not only our pets, but they are the livelihoods of many. Just like with human medicine, we have to study animals to know how to care for them, treat them, and keep them healthy."

"And the protesters?" he asked, his eyes holding concern.

"I get it," she said, her voice rising slightly. "Chester Thompson is a rancher, and he cares about his land and his stock. He wants to make sure that it's safe." She sucked in a ragged breath and dropped her gaze to the side for a moment, gathering her thoughts. Lifting her chin, she stared directly into Eric's face, and continued. "But he does not understand, or accept, that the study going on at the NBAF is so secure, that his protests are foundless."

"During her introduction, Dr. Hughley was explaining that all the floors that go deep underground are where the dangerous diseases are studied."

Nodding, Lydia agreed. "The facility was built with every precaution in mind. It's like the sci-fi movie, Andromeda Strain. What I do with the healthy animals is on the ground level, but there are five levels deep into the ground, each level with its own containment system. The job that I do is to simply work with healthy animals and make sure that they continue to be healthy. I draw blood from them to be used in research, no different than when a human has blood drawn for testing. But to someone like Chester, his protest began in the typical way. Signs, chanting, writing letters to Congressman. I feel that now that the NBAF is functional and working, he's stepping up his protests and getting nasty." Shrugging, she added, "That's his right, but I don't have to like it."

"And when you saw me with him, that hit a nerve."

She nodded and sighed again. "Yes, and looking back, that was unfair of me. We had a night with no expectations beyond and certainly didn't divulge anything personal. So, it was completely irrational of me to have become angry when you were just doing your job. For that, I truly am sorry. I can't even explain why I reacted so badly." Another sigh slipped from her lips, and she added, "As I mentioned earlier, my life has had some big changes recently, and I suppose I've been a bit more emotional. That's not a good excuse, just a reason."

Eric's gaze drifted over to the opposite wall, where several framed pictures were hung. Lydia turned her head and followed his line of vision. She smiled, and said, "That's my pride and joy. My daughter, Caroline. She recently left for college for the first time. So, it's just me now."

1 2

Eric had been on pins and needles walking up to Lydia's door, not knowing what her reaction was going to be. When she had finally let him in and invited him to stay for dinner, he jumped at the chance to do whatever it took to stay in her presence.

Her house was small and simply furnished, and he wondered if she had been living there long. The entryway opened directly into the living room and to the right was an area that had probably been intended for a small dining room but was being used as an office. A desk, complete with laptop, printer, and various papers and magazines piled on top, sat in the corner. A comfortable chair next to a floor lamp completed the space.

Her kitchen was an eat-in, with a small table at the window overlooking the yard. Now that the meal was finished and they were ensconced in the living room, Eric hoped Lydia would continue to share about her life. She seemed incapable of holding a grudge and had not only apologized, which was something he had not been seeking, but she had begun to talk, and he loved hearing about her work.

Now, as she mentioned her daughter, he watched her face light up in a smile, and he wanted to keep that smile on her face.

"Jim mentioned that you had a daughter in college, but it's hard to believe. You must have had her very young."

Her eyes widened, and she said, "I can't imagine why Jim would mention that!" She chuckled and fiddled with the hem of her shirt. "But I suppose I talk about her a lot."

"Tell me about her." Lydia's gaze jumped back to his, doubt in her eyes, and he said, "Really. I'd love to hear about her."

Her smile brightened her face again, and she said, "I was young when I had her. My high school boyfriend, Tim, worked in his father's garage. He was two years older than me, and by the time I was a senior, he was already making decent money as a mechanic. Of course, typical teenage hormones took over, and we were not as responsible as we should have been. I got pregnant just before my eighteenth birthday, right when I graduated from high school. I know you might think that our families would have been very disappointed in us, but both sets were happy to be having a grandchild."

"So, you had Caroline when you were only eighteen. No wonder you look so young...you are young."

Laughing, she said, "I'll be thirty-nine on my next birthday."

"And, Tim?" Part of him hated to ask, but he really wanted to know what happened with Caroline's father.

"Oh, we got married and, against the odds, we were very happy. I actually got a job as a receptionist in a veterinarian's office, and Tim continued to work for his dad. We weren't rich, but we did fine. I gave birth to Caroline, and she was the light of our lives. Between our two moms, we saved a lot of money on childcare, put money down on a little house, and I thought all of my dreams had come true. Of course, life has a way of giving and other times jerking the rug right out from underneath you."

Eric held his breath, uncertain what was coming next. The chair Lydia was sitting in was close to the sofa and he leaned forward, taking her hand in his. "You don't have to tell me."

Holding his gaze, Lydia shook her head slowly. "I know that's not what we are to each other…you know, confidants."

"That's not what I meant. I would love to know, but only if you want to tell me."

She hesitated, and he wondered if she was going to continue to speak. He found himself wanting to know and gave her hand a little squeeze, hoping to communicate how much he yearned to have her share more with him. As though understanding his silent request, she nodded.

"Tim and his dad were out one day in the snow and ice, going to tow a car that had gotten stuck in a snowbank. A dump truck skidded on the ice going around a curve and slammed into them. They were both killed instantly."

"I'm so sorry," he said, hating the sadness in her voice. "You must have been devastated."

Nodding, she said, "I lost my husband and my father-in-law at the same time. And, essentially, I lost my mother-in-law as well. She's still living but is a shell of the woman that she was, never having moved on after losing her husband and son. But I had Caroline to live for, and my daughter is what had me continue to get up and function on the days that I wanted to pull the covers over my head. I had hoped that Caroline would be able to do that for my mother-in-law as well, but I don't think anything can really reach her."

"Is that when you decided to become a veterinarian?"

Nodding, she said, "Yes. The veterinarian that I worked for encouraged me to go to school. So, I went to the local community college and became a vet tech, so that I could make more money since I was now a single parent. I did that for a few years, and then went back to school to get my undergraduate degree in biology while still working. As soon as I had that, I applied to VetMed schools. That meant that Caroline and I had to move, which was hard because my parents had continued to be my support system. Caroline was ten years old at the time, but thankfully I was accepted to the closest school possible, so my parents were still able to be involved in her life."

Shaking his head, Eric was filled with admiration

and humbled at her willingness to move forward in the face of such devastation.

"So, there's not much more to tell."

"You sum those years up so succinctly, but I can't imagine that any of that was easy."

She shook her head and smiled. "No, it wasn't easy. Money was tight. I had set aside the insurance money from Tim's death for Caroline's college fund. Since she was so young at the time he died, the money has had a chance to be invested, and she can now go to college debt-free. I confess that I had to use a little bit for me, but with grants and some scholarships, I was able to take care of most of my college needs. I worked for several years and finally paid off all loans. I was given a stipend for my internship, and when I accepted the job here at NBAF, good money and benefits finally started rolling in."

"So, for the first time in your life, money is not an issue but now your daughter's gone." He said the words, meaning to show his understanding, but as soon as they left his mouth, he spied the tears gathering in her eyes. "Oh, Lydia, I'm so sorry. I didn't mean to say anything insensitive."

Lydia chuckled even as she lifted her hand to wipe a stray tear. "Goodness, Eric, it's not you. It's just been Caroline and me for so long. As a parent, you raise your child to be independent and, yet, when they become that way, you miss them."

Shaking her head, as though to clear her mind, she said, "This is ridiculous. I've done nothing but talk about me the entire time you've been here. Tell me about yourself."

Guilt stabbed him as he viewed her guileless face. He had wanted to see her again, wanted to know more about her, and his visit this evening had accomplished that. She was as beautiful on the inside as she was on the outside, and his admiration for her had increased beyond his imaginings. And now? She was waiting for him to explain his life and how he had become a journalist. *Fuck. I should've just left things alone.* To stay and continue talking would only exacerbate the lie and, while it was his mission, he no longer liked the pretense.

Eric moved his hand away from hers and offered a self-deprecating shrug. "There's not much to tell, definitely not a moving story like yours." He glanced at his watch and faked surprise at the time. "Oh, wow, I'm sorry. I had no idea it was getting so late, and we both have to get up tomorrow for work." He stood, trying to ignore the hurt that passed through her eyes.

Jumping to her feet, Lydia began walking toward the door. Suddenly stopping, she whirled around, and he had to come to a quick halt to keep from running into her. Her eyes searched his and she rushed out, "Would you like to stay the night?"

Multiple thoughts ran through his mind, slamming into each other. He wanted to shout 'yes' from the top of his lungs but knew it would be unfair to her. Chivalry won out, but as though she knew what he was about to say, she rushed in again.

"It's only a night, Eric. I don't need to know anything

more about you. I don't need to know your background, your job, your history. I know you'll be leaving in a few days and, honestly, right now, that's fine with me. I'm not looking for a man. I'm not looking for a relationship. But you were right earlier when you said what we had was a good thing. It was special, and it's been a long time since I've had special. So, if you're willing for just one more night, I'd love to have you stay."

His eyes devoured her face and he saw nothing but sincerity staring back at him. He knew he should walk out the door but could not deny how much he wanted her. To hold her again for just one more night. It was a risk, maybe more to him than her considering he knew they would be making love, not fucking. But at that moment he could not deny her request. After all, it was his deepest desire, as well.

Eric lifted his hands, placing them softly on either side of her jaw, with his fingers sweeping back her hair and his thumbs caressing her cheeks. He pulled her gently toward him until their bodies were aligned and her head was tilted back as she held his gaze. He did not take his eyes from hers, but felt her hands slide from his waist to around his back, her fingers gripping his shirt.

He bent his head, angling slightly so their noses would not bump, and said, "There's nowhere else I'd rather be tonight, than here with you, in your arms."

Lydia's lips curved into a smile that shot straight to his heart. Leaning forward the final inch, he settled his lips over hers. The feel, the texture, the taste was every bit as sweet as he remembered. As he moved his lips over hers, she opened her mouth, and he felt her slight sigh down to his gut. He slid his tongue into her mouth, gently memorizing every crevice, thinking to take it slow. But she had other ideas, and her fingers gripped his shirt tightly as her tongue began to tangle with his.

The feeling of her tongue dancing wildly with his shot straight to his cock, which was already pressing against his jeans at the thought of another night spent with her. His fingertips on the back of her head held her tightly as he plundered the depths of her mouth, seeking and finding every glorious nuance. Her breasts pressed against his chest, and as he lowered one hand to slide down her back, her hips pressed in, creating an unbelievable need.

Lifting his head, he dragged in a raspy breath, stunned that this woman could kiss in a way that made him think of nothing but getting her naked and horizontal. Her eyes stared back at him, glassy and unfocused, as though the kiss had been a drug to her as well.

"Bed."

He only managed to utter one word and was glad when she understood his meaning. With a quick nod, she stepped back and linked fingers with his. Just past the kitchen was a short hall, three doors opening from it. He assumed one, the small second bedroom, was probably for Caroline when she came home to visit. The other would be a bathroom, and the third door, the one she led him through, was a small master bedroom with its own adjoining bathroom.

That was the only observation he managed before his eyes alighted on the bed, and his brain short-circuited to anything other than getting her on it.

Whatever switch had been flipped with Lydia, as soon as they walked into her bedroom, she went even wilder. Before he had a chance to make the move himself, she whipped her shirt over her head, baring her torso, her breasts covered in a light pink satin bra. He grinned as she slid her thumbs into the waistband of her sweatpants and shucked them off her legs, kicking them to the side.

Glancing down, she chuckled before lifting her gaze and saying, "I can't believe that, for once, my bra matches my panties."

Barely registering her words as his gaze moved from head to toe, he finally landed back on her face, and asked, "Is that actually a thing?"

Nodding, she said, "Yeah, I suppose so. At least, for some women it's important."

"All I want to do is get you naked so I can't imagine that your bra and panties matching would ever make any difference. Quite honestly, I can't imagine any guy giving a fuck, because the only thing a guy wants is to get the girl naked."

Her eyes widened as another chuckle slipped from her kiss-swollen lips. "Well, I guess that's honest," she admitted, "but, I think there's a lot of women that would be very disappointed in that."

"Baby, if you're dressed, everything underneath is still left to the man's imagination. If a man ever gets a woman to the point where she's standing in front of him in just a bra and panties, he's only a second away from learning whether or not his imagination did her justice. Basically, he doesn't care what they look like."

Lydia planted her hands on her hips and tilted her head to the side, "So I could be wearing a white, cotton bra and granny panties, and you wouldn't care?"

"Babe," he said, jerking his shirt over his head, grinning as he watched her gaze drop down over his torso. "I can't believe we're having this conversation right now, but yeah...you could be in an old bra and ratty underwear and I wouldn't give a fuck, because they'd be coming off in about two seconds."

To prove his point, he stepped forward and, with the flip of his fingers, undid her bra. As her breasts were freed, he lifted one and bent to suckle, causing her to gasp as her hands gripped his shoulders.

He moved from one breast to the other, sucking each nipple deep, then hooked his thumbs in her panties and shoved them down over her hips as far as he could reach. Her breasts jiggled as her body bounced slightly in her effort to kick her panties off her feet.

Standing up, he slowly moved his gaze from her beautiful face down to her generous curves, all the way to her painted toenails. Dragging his gaze back up to her face, he grinned. "Now, *that*, is the prize I want, no matter what packaging might be around it."

13

Lydia's gaze dropped to Eric's jeans and she said, "You're not the only one who likes what's under the packaging."

Throwing his head back in laughter, his hands went to his zipper, and as he stepped out of his jeans and boxers, he bent to retrieve his wallet.

"Don't just pull out one," she said, laughing at the wide-eyed expression on his face. "If this is to be our final night together, let's make it last."

He pulled out several condoms and tossed them to the bed before turning toward her, his fist encircling his cock. "You want it, babe, you've got it."

Watching his hand move up and down his cock, she felt the air rush from her lungs, "Oh, yeah, I want it." She almost did not recognize her voice, her words raspy with need. She dropped to her knees and licked the drop of pre-cum, hearing a hiss leave his lips. He reached out, burying his fingertips in her thick hair as she slid her mouth over the tip, tonguing the sensitive rim. This time, the hiss was accompanied by a, "Fuck", and she grinned while taking as much of him as she could.

She worked his cock with her mouth, bobbing up and down, gliding her tongue along the ridges, changing her speed, and adding just enough suction that he swelled even more. With the heady experience of knowing how much pleasure she was giving this strong man, she desired to make him feel as good as he had made her feel the other night.

Suddenly, his cock was no longer in her mouth and he bent, snagged her up under her arms and, as though she weighed nothing, gave her a gentle toss back onto the bed.

She pouted, "I wasn't finished."

"I come, I come inside you."

Her nostrils flared as the pout dropped from her face, desire overriding everything. Lying on her back, she reached her hand down and drew it through her slick folds, circling her clit. "Then by all means, come on," she invited.

He crawled onto the bed, his eyes glued to her hand on her sex. "Now, you're being a tease."

A grin was her only reply as she opened her legs wider. He rolled on the condom, then replaced her hand with his, and she knew he would find her ready. Holding his body up with his right hand planted on the mattress near her, he positioned his cock at her entrance, moving the tip, gathering her juices.

He shifted his hips forward, impaling her, and a gasp left her lips at the fullness. She wrapped her legs around his waist, her heels urging him forward as they dug into his muscular ass. He took her hint and began thrusting, slow to begin with and then faster, building the friction they both craved.

Her hands wrapped around him, first clutching his waist and then sliding up to his shoulders, feeling his muscles bunch and tighten with every movement. There was such power in his body and yet he handled her with such gentleness.

She knew what this was…just one more night, but she did not care. She wanted this, she wanted this man and, if one more night was all she could have, she would take it gladly. For the first time in a long time, she felt like a woman. Not a mom, or a daughter, or a veterinarian, or an employee…just a desirable woman.

She felt the cusp of her orgasm as her inner muscles tightened and heat moved across her body. As she shuddered through her release, she kept her eyes open, not wanting to miss one second of seeing his face as his body moved into hers.

She did not have to wait long, for with a few more thrusts he followed her with his own release, his head thrown back and her name leaving his lips. That, she supposed, was the sweetest sound of all.

After a moment's respite, with his arms circled around her, he slowly climbed from the bed and headed to the bathroom. She rolled to one side, admiring his body both going and coming into the room. She threw back the covers, silently inviting him to stay. Her heart leaped as he grinned and joined her.

"I know you have to go back to your hotel to change clothes tomorrow, but will you stay with me tonight? We can set the alarm, to give you plenty of time."

His hand lifted to brush damp tendrils of hair away from her face, and he smiled. "Yeah, babe, I'd like to stay. After all, I've got more condoms to use."

Laughing, she said, "Then I guess we'd better get busy."

Lydia awoke with the feeling of warm heat at her back. It took no time for her to remember the reason for that warmth, considering the tingle she still felt between her legs. She wondered if it would be feasible for her to call in sick, shut off the alarm, and continue to lay wrapped in Eric's arms. That thought was dangerous, though...he would be leaving soon.

Refusing to give in to that idea, she took the time she did have to snuggle deeper. After a moment, she felt him shifting, his warm lips soft against her neck. "It's not time to get up yet," she said.

His breath whispered by her ear. "That's too bad, 'cause I'm already up."

He pressed his hips forward, and she felt his morning wood against her ass. "Mmm," she mumbled and lifted her leg, allowing him entrance.

He thrust from the back, with one hand wrapped

under, fondling her breast, and the other hand cupping her mound, fingering her clit. It only took a moment for her to cry out his name, and he soon followed with his own orgasm.

Lying on the bed, feeling boneless, she gave voice to her earlier thought. "Think we can get away with calling in sick today and just stay here?" As soon as the words were out of her mouth, she hated hearing the neediness.

He quickly set her mind at ease, nibbling on her shoulder and saying, "God, I wish we could. There's nowhere I'd rather be than right here with you, spending the whole day in bed."

Lydia twisted around so that she could face him, her hand cupping his stubbled jaw and sleep-tousled hair. Leaning forward she kissed him, wanting to pour her emotions into the kiss, and yet holding back.

"Does it have to end right now?" he asked.

Her eyes widened, surprised to find that his train of thought was so similar to hers. "Not on my account," she confessed. "As far as I'm concerned, we can continue to see each other as long as you're in town."

Eric's smile was wide, and she answered with one of her own. Just then, her alarm rang and they both fell onto their backs, groaning. She climbed out of bed first, saying, "Let me take a quick shower, and then you can have one while I'm getting ready. That way, you only have to change your clothes when you get back to your hotel. I can even fix some breakfast here."

He reached out and grabbed her hand, halting her progress. She looked down at him, curious, and he suggested, "How about we shower together, I'll give you time to get ready, and then we can have breakfast at my hotel. Then you can leave for work, and I'll have just enough time to change clothes."

She thought for just a moment, then decided she liked his plan. With a wink and a grin, she tugged him from the bed, and they headed to the shower.

An hour later, they had finished breakfast and said their goodbyes so that Eric could go to his room and Lydia could go to work. He watched her drive away after a gentle kiss in the parking lot. The morning had been one of the best he could remember. Waking up with a woman he cared about, morning sex, and then more fooling around in the shower together.

Lydia had said he made her self-conscious while she put on her makeup and fixed her hair, but he found that he did not want to waste a moment with her. Even something so mundane seemed strangely comforting to him. Since his divorce many years ago, he had not considered his bachelorhood to be lonely. But now, it seemed as though Lydia filled an empty place deep inside of himself that he had not known existed.

Jogging back to his room, he opened the door and spied Chris sitting on his couch wearing a T-shirt that proclaimed *Geek: computer whisperer* across the chest. He was munching a breakfast bagel, with his feet up on the coffee table, while balancing his laptop on his lap.

"Do you always make yourself at home in other people's rooms?" he quipped.

Chewing and swallowing before answering, Chris said, "Well, hell, it's not like you're using your room. Saw you and the pretty veterinarian having breakfast. You were making such googly eyes at each other, you didn't even see me come in to get my bagel."

In a good mood having spent the night with Lydia, Eric ignored Chris and grabbed clean clothes out of his closet. Heading into the bathroom, he took care of his business, changed clothes, and walked out, seeing Chris still there. Lifting his eyebrow, he asked, "You got anything new for me?"

"I've figured out the coordinates of where the animal extremist group took you." Wiggling his eyebrows, Chris added, "How's that for a pop in your Rice Crispies?"

Eyes already narrowed in thought, he turned around and nodded. "What'll it take for us to get in there?"

Chris' smile drooped as he remarked, "That's the part I don't know how to do. I might can tinker enough with their security to be able to get you in, but I'm just not sure."

Hands on his hips, he ran through several scenarios in his mind. Finally, he pulled out his phone and placed a call. "Mace? It's Eric Lopez. Think you're up for little business from DHS through me?" Chuckling, he listened as Mace gave an unequivocal 'hell yeah'. "I've got a building that's undoubtedly secure that I need to get into. The people I'm investigating are seriously nasty customers, and I'm sure they've got security out the wazoo. If your computer and security gurus can get the information from my guy here, can they take a look and see if I can get in and out undetected?"

He listened for another minute, and then said, "Got it. And thanks, man. You can bill us, or I'll owe you a marker. Hell, even if you bill DHS, I'll still owe you a marker and a bottle of the finest Scotch whiskey I can get."

Disconnecting, Eric looked at Chris who was now sitting up straight, eyes wide, obviously impressed.

"Damn, man, you don't fuck around. Can I even ask who that was, or would you have to kill me?" Chris asked.

"Jesus," he said, shaking his head, unable to keep from grinning at Chris' antics. "A former SEAL buddy of mine now works for a security company based out of New England. Lighthouse Security Investigations. Mace is the boss, and I helped him out with a case recently. He said if I ever needed assistance to let them know, and I figured now was as good a time as any."

"You just tell me what I need to do, and I'll get it done."

"Send everything you've got through this secure channel," he instructed, handing him the information scribbled on a piece of paper. "They've got people who work for them that can shut down security systems, allowing someone to get in and do an investigation. They can even alter the security cameras so that the FLA will never know anything happened."

Eyes wide once again, Chris shook his head. "I'm

good, but there's a lot I've got to learn to be able to do that. But I'm young. Never fear, I'll learn."

Laughing, he slipped his shoes on and shoved his wallet and keys into his pockets. "I don't doubt it, Chris. But, for now, just keep getting me what I need."

14

It was Lydia's last day with the journalists. Actually, last half day since they would be rejoining the scientists for the final day and a half of the seminar. The scientists, who had been to some of the research areas of the NBAF, would inform their own country's journalists with what they deemed necessary for them to know and report on.

She had been looking forward to getting back to her regular duties, but as Eric walked into the room, she wished they had more time together. Jim had taken the group over to the bovine section, and they had a tour of the Veterinary Medical School at KSU. Now, they were back with her to finish their discussion about African Swine Fever and prevention. Attempting to ignore the heated look Eric was giving her from the back of the room, she turned to the others.

"I know that you have been immersed in our discussions of healthy swine as well as some of the swine diseases, particularly focusing on African Swine Fever. Information is vital to protecting animals as well as humans. The articles that you write when you return to your individual countries will play a great role in dispersing such pivotal information.

"Basic disease transmission prevention between animals and humans is very similar to what you would expect from human to human contact. For example, farmers should not have direct contact with their pigs if they have been in contact with someone else's pigs within the previous twenty-four hours. Limit the access of rodents and wildlife where the swine are located. Quarantine is extremely important. New animals arriving on a farm should be quarantined for at least seven days.

"The cleaning and disinfecting of all equipment between uses, is also highly effective in keeping down the transmission of diseases. That includes feeders, waterers, and certainly any veterinary equipment."

Nodding to Jim, he began handing out packets of information, telling them that they were allowed to use direct quotations from anything that was given to them.

"Personal protective equipment is also needed. When you first met me, I was wearing rubber boots, gloves, and scrubs." She paused, and then laughed, "Of course, I was also wearing some fashionable mud."

The others laughed with her, and she looked over as Eric winked at her. Trying to ignore the skip in her heartbeat, she walked back over to her computer, pulling up more information. "At this time, Jim and I will take individual questions."

Eric watched as the others compared notes and chatted amongst themselves, as well as speaking to Lydia and Jim. After a few minutes, Ji-Ho cornered Lydia, monopolizing her attention. Any time one of the other journalists came by, Ji-Ho would shift his body, blocking them from Lydia and forcing them to move toward Jim to get their question answered.

He watched this for several minutes, fighting the urge to walk over and shove the other man away, claiming Lydia for himself. Knowing he had to keep that emotion in check, he continued to watch the others as he pretended to listen to Jim.

Egor and Wang had formed an interesting alliance, standing to the side of the lab area talking lowly between themselves. Anong made her way over to him and engaged him in conversation, shifting away when Bashiir came by.

Looking back toward Lydia, he observed Ji-Ho leaning into her personal space as he continued to ply her with questions. Unable to take it anymore, he walked over, clapped his hand on Ji-Ho's shoulder, and said, "You need to let someone else have a chance to get Dr. Hughes' opinion." Without giving Ji-Ho a chance to respond, he stepped forward, capturing Lydia's attention.

The next hour passed uneventfully, and he was glad when the group was called to break for lunch. Stepping out with the others, he made sure to be at the back of the line. Looking over his shoulder, he winked and grinned, seeing Lydia smile back in return.

After Eric closed the door, Lydia plopped into a chair. She was thrilled to be alone, since Jim was in charge of escorting them to the cafeteria and then he and Beth would have lunch. It had been interesting to host visitors, and she knew it was an honor to have been chosen as one of the NBAF employees tasked with guiding the journalists through the conference. But, at the same time, it was exhausting.

Having eaten a large breakfast that morning with Eric, she quickly ate her yogurt before deciding to go back into the animal area. Donning her lab coat, boots, and gloves, she walked into the swine housing. Squeals and grunts met her ears, and she checked on the piglets first, before moving to the next pen of older sows. The animals came to her, grunting in pleasure as she scratched behind their ears.

"You girls don't have to worry about finding someone special, do you?" One large sow ambled closer, looking up at her as though she understood the question.

She laughed, and said, "No, girl, you don't. You find a mate easily and then have a litter of piglets." She leaned down and scratched behind both ears at the same time, laughing at the grunts coming her way.

"You always spend your lunch time talking to pigs?"

Startled, she jumped at the deep, but familiar, voice

coming from behind her. Twisting around, she spied Eric standing at the outside of the gate, a wide smile on his handsome face. "What are you doing in here?"

"It was a choice between lunch with a diverse, interesting group of journalists who are now paired back with their corresponding scientists or come to find you with the pigs."

Laughing, she said, "And given those choices, you chose the pigs?"

His smile deepened, but he did not laugh, as he replied, "No. I chose you."

She stood speechless, uncertain of his full meaning and not wanting to embarrass herself by making any assumptions.

As though reading her mind, he added, "But, choosing you also means I choose the pigs."

She laughed again and walked toward the gate. He gallantly unlatched it for her, and she moved through, turning to secure the gate behind her. Looking up at him, her breath caught in her throat as his eyes bore straight into hers.

"Should I be concerned?" he asked. At her quizzical expression, he explained further. "Concerned that you're seeking the company of the pigs after being with all of us?"

"Ah." They fell in step together, walking back toward the lab, and she said, truthfully, "No. I just have to confess that, after the noise of so many people being around, I like my solitude. Or, at least the company of the pigs who are not constantly badgering me with scientific questions."

"I like the quiet also," he admitted.

"That must be hard for a journalist," she surmised. "You must have to constantly be around people."

He cast a quick smile her way, but she noted it did not reach his eyes. Curious, she remained silent as they walked back into the lab area. She hosed down her boots and slid them off, pulling off the outer scrubs as well as the gloves and putting them in the disposal unit.

"Is that what Ji-Ho was doing? Badgering you with scientific questions?"

Her forehead scrunched in thought, and then she shook her head slowly. "Not necessarily. At first, he had several questions specific to swine and various diseases, but then his questions became more...varied."

"Varied?" he asked, his voice carrying an edge.

Wondering if he was perhaps jealous, she assured, "Nothing personal. Just questions that were more about the security of the NBAF."

"They covered what we were supposed to know in the large meetings. I can't imagine what else Ji-Ho wanted to know."

"He was asking about some of the employees with the higher security clearances. Questions like how they got them, what floors they worked on, if most of them lived in this area, if DHS brought them here." She looked at him, and said, "They didn't make any sense to me, and I told him several times that I could not answer those questions. That's when I was glad you came over and elbowed him out of the way."

She watched Eric's face transform with anger, but before they had a chance to speak further, Jim and Beth came back into the lab from lunch. Their gazes shot to Eric, before moving over to her.

Eric grinned and held up the file in his hand. "Realized I got to lunch and had left this here." Turning to her, he said, "Dr. Hughes, thanks for answering my questions. It's been very enlightening being around you for the past several days." With a nod to Beth and Jim, he moved out of the room.

Jim held her gaze for a moment, but she said nothing. Hearing Beth sigh, she looked over and the young woman said, "Good God, that man is gorgeous. Don't you agree, Lydia?"

She stammered, caught off guard. "Sure...uh...yeah, sure." Hoping her coworkers did not see the pink filling her cheeks, she turned back to her desk and began to work.

Unable to have his phone with him while in the NBAF, Eric walked immediately to his car and called Chris. "Focus your efforts on Ji-Ho," he barked.

"Righty-oh, boss," Chris responded. "Anything special he's been up to?"

"Just found out he got very chatty with Dr. Hughes today, and his questions were not in line with what he should have been asking scientifically. He seemed to be drilling her about the security of this facility and those who have a high-level security clearance."

"Fuck. Okay, I've been focusing on him anyway, but I'll double down. Since I've been in contact with Lighthouse Security's computer people, you want me to get them to work on him as well?"

"Abso-fucking-lutely," Eric replied. "I trust my instincts and your abilities, but I was told I could form my own team, and right now, I'm teaming up with Mace's Lighthouse Security group."

"You got it."

"One last thing, Chris. If anything comes up tonight, you know how to get hold of me. I probably won't be in my room."

"No worries," Chris said, just before disconnecting.

He was pleased that Chris did not feel like cracking a joke about him spending time with Lydia. While he knew his partner needed to know where he was, his relationship with her was too special to be bandied about by anyone.

Locking his car and setting the security, he headed back into the building to keep an eye on the rest of the journalists, as they were now in the final phases of the seminar. But what he was really looking forward to, was the upcoming evening with Lydia.

15

"Hey,"

Eric held his phone to his ear and stared down at his boots, a smile playing about his lips. Hearing Lydia's soft 'hey' made him want to be with her even more. "Hey, back," he said. Sighing, he continued, "I really wanted to take you to dinner tonight, but I'm going to have to take a rain check. I've got something that I'm gonna have to take care of, and I don't know when I'll get back."

He hoped she would not ask more questions, because he hated lying to her any more than he already was. He heard the hesitation and held his breath.

"Oh, okay. Well, will you be gone all night?"

Not having any idea how long his night's mission was going to take, he replied truthfully, "I don't know. My boss needs me to go out of town to check on something, and I can't be sure when I'll get back."

MARYANN JORDAN

"Oh, okay," she repeated, and he could hear the disappointment in her voice.

"I'm really sorry, Lydia, because there's nowhere I'd rather be than with you."

Her voice firmer now, she said, "It's fine, Eric. I understand what we have, and it's okay for us to—"

"No, don't say it." He dragged his hand through his hair, frustration pouring off of him. "This is nothing more than me having to take on another job that's gonna run into the evening. Please, don't think it has anything to do with you or what we have. If I get in tonight, and it's not terribly late, can I come by?"

"Absolutely," she said, relief evident in her voice. "I can't leave my door unlocked, but I always sleep with my phone next to me, so you can call if you're able to head on over." She hesitated before adding, "And if not, then I'll see you—"

"Tomorrow. If I can't come tonight, then you'll see me tomorrow, and I'll take you to dinner. Promise," he added.

"Eric, please don't promise things that you might not be able to keep. It's okay. I'm a big girl and can handle what we've got. So, if you can come tonight, do. And if not, then we'll try to have dinner tomorrow."

Sighing, he glanced over as Chris came into his room, bouncing on his toes with excitement. "Okay, I'll see you as soon as I can." Disconnecting, he tossed his phone to his bed, pinching the bridge of his nose with his forefinger and thumb. Closing his eyes for a moment to re-center his thoughts on the mission, he inhaled deeply, then let the air out slowly.

Lifting his head, he looked at Chris, and asked, "Are we set?"

Chris nodded, his red hair standing on end, as though he had run his fingers through it one time too many. "I've been working with two of Mace's men, Josh and Clay. I gotta tell you, I'm good at what I do but after spending hours working with them, well…let's just say that I want to be them when I grow up!"

Mentally rolling his eyes, he pinned Chris with a hard stare. "Just tell me what I need to do and how it's going to be accomplished."

"Okay, okay," Chris said, moving over and sitting down on the sofa. "Using the coordinates that I was able to gather from your tracer, we've pinpointed the exact building that you were taken to. While they did not find any tracer on you, they did have a jamming system that was keeping me from getting a clear signal. Josh and Clay were able to un-jam whatever the extremists were using. So, once they knew the building, they were able to figure out its security and how to get around it."

Sitting down in the chair facing the sofa, he leaned forward with his forearms resting on his knees. His interest piqued, he had to admit he loved this part of the mission. The covert action that always resulted in an adrenaline rush, knowing that he was battling an enemy. "Ready."

"You and I are going to drive there tonight. When we're five miles out, I'll contact Josh and Clay, and they'll be ready. Remotely, Clay can shut down their security so that we can get into the building. He'll be able to reset any of their cameras so there will be no record of our being there and no skip in the timestamp. Once we get anything we can from their computers, I'll transmit it through the portal that Josh has given me. He'll start running analysis on it, and I'll do the same when we get back. Anything I'm not sure about, he's going to go over with me."

"We?" Seeing Chris' lowered brow, Eric continued, "You said we. *We* will go into the building."

"Yeah. We, as in both of us. You know, you and me…we."

Throwing his head back, he said, "Jesus, Chris. I know what the word *we* means. What I don't know is why there is a *we*. You haven't been in the field enough to be able to deal with breaking into a building."

Chris sucked in a deep breath before letting it out slowly. "Eric, man, I know I'm new at this, but I'm ready. Normally, I wouldn't be going in so that I could be on the outside feeding you whatever information I needed to. But, in this case, we'll have Josh and Clay doing that."

"Yes, and they're in Maine, not fuckin' Kansas."

"It doesn't matter where they are. They're monitoring all the security, including the perimeter. I don't even know how they do all of that, but they can, and they will. That gives me the chance to be on the inside with you. Two people working the inside will go faster than one."

He fought the urge to demand that Chris stay on the outside. Instead, he looked at the eager face of the agent in front of him and flashed back to the first mission he was on. He may have been a SEAL, but he remembered the eager anticipation of getting that first mission under his belt.

Nodding slowly, he said, "Don't make me fuckin' regret doing this, but okay—"

Chris jumped up and waved his hands above his head. "You won't, you won't, I promise."

"Don't promise something that you might not be able to keep." He recognized that he had just repeated Lydia's words and shook his head slowly. Focusing back on Chris, he ordered, "You'll do everything I say and not one thing more or less. You got that? 'Cause if you don't, this'll be the last chance at a mission you'll ever get."

Chris nodded solemnly. "You won't regret this. I'll give you everything you need for this to be successful, and then we can get what we collect to Josh and Clay, who will help me analyze it."

"Then go change. Black shirt, black pants, black jacket, black socks, black shoes, and please, God, tell me you've got a black cap that can cover your red hair!"

So far, so good.

Eric knew the success of missions was due in large part to extensive planning and trust in your fellow team members. Part of SEAL training was spending time together twenty-four–seven. This forced the team to get to know each other, anticipate each other's moves, understand nonverbal communication, and instinctively know where every member of your team was at all times. It also meant that you had absolute trust that each member of the team would be able to improvise as the mission progressed.

Now, he was working with a team he did not know. He had never met Josh or Clay but had to trust what he knew about the Lighthouse Security Investigations company. He knew that Mace had been former Army Special Forces and a CIA Special Operator. He also knew that Mace had filled his company with other military Special Operators. But, placing his trust in people he had never worked with before took a leap of faith.

Chris was another matter. He trusted Chris doing all of the background work and the on-site security, but he was untried in the field. Anything could happen. Glancing at him now, Chris was no longer his usual exuberant self but appeared to be quietly focused. Not knowing him well enough, he could not tell if that was due to nerves, determination, or just plain wishing he were somewhere else. Sighing, he considered asking Chris to stay behind in the car, but if Clay successfully shut down the security, the extra pair of hands would be good.

Even with all that on his mind, he still had to consider that part of a mission's success was due to luck. He just hoped his held as he and Chris made their way through the building.

Just as planned, they had stopped approximately five miles from their destination and contacted Josh. Once Clay had disabled all outer security measures the FLA had, they moved forward, parking far away from the building. Both dressed in all black, they moved silently toward one of the back doors.

Once he received the signal from Josh that Clay had disabled the security of the building, including the inside, he moved them through the door. He had gone over the instructions with Chris numerous times and was pleased to see that he was following them to the letter.

Using night vision goggles, he led the way down a long hall. The building was only one story and the inside was void of any personality. No pictures on the wall, no carpet, no indication of what went on inside at all. There were several doors standing open from the hall. Peering into the first one, it looked like the room in which he had been taken. It still held the same empty desk and two chairs that had been there previously. Stepping across the hall, they entered what appeared to be a real office. With a nod toward Chris, he indicated for him to download all of the information from the computer. As Chris went to work, Eric took the opportunity to look through the office.

Using a special lamp that would illuminate fingerprints, he found several clear sets on the desk. Pulling out strips of special fingerprint lifting tape, he collected the samples, not being encumbered with using dusting powder. Slipping those into his pocket, he moved over to a filing cabinet and unlocked it easily but found it to be mostly empty. Flipping through a few of the files, he snapped pictures, not taking the time to examine each one.

Chris indicated that he was finished with the computer, and they slipped back out of the room. There were three other rooms that they examined, two other offices and what appeared to be a workroom. He noted few furnishings and nothing personal from anyone who might be working there. He could see the question in Chris' eyes, but shook his head, having warned him not to speak while they were in the building.

After Chris had extracted all the data that he could from the computers and, sending a signal to Josh, they moved back out of the building, securing it as before. Stealthily walking through the darkness back to their vehicle, they drove away, once more alerting Clay to re-secure the building behind them.

They drove in silence for several miles, Chris unusually quiet in the passenger seat. Not used to asking a team member how they were doing, Eric nonetheless looked to the side as they drove back to Manhattan. "You okay?"

"Yeah, yeah," Chris said, his voice strangely unanimated.

They continued in silence for several more miles, and then Chris finally said, "Was that good? I mean, was that a normal mission?"

Unsure what Chris was getting at, he replied, "Yeah, that was good. We got in, we got what we came for, we got out. That's about the best a mission can go." Turning to look at Chris again, he asked, "Why?"

"I don't know. I guess I just thought I'd be more elated. I was excited about going in, but then, to be perfectly honest, I was nervous as fuck when we got in there. Then we got out, and I don't know that we actually, really got anything important for all our trouble."

"Right now, I'm just pleased as fuck we got in and

got out," Eric told him. "I did get some fingerprints, which I'll send back to DHS, and you'll send the computer information to Josh and Clay."

"You're right," Chris agreed, sighing heavily. "I think being a little scared probably just surprised me."

He heard the sound of defeat in Chris' voice, and added, "Look, Chris, you did good. I was worried, but you did everything I asked. And, I have to admit, with you going in with me, we were able to get things done a lot quicker. For a job like this, quick is best."

Thirty minutes later, they pulled up to the hotel, and Chris' good mood had returned. Looking over at him, Chris grinned widely. "This job has been my first real taste of fieldwork and tonight was my first real adventure on a mission. Thanks, man." Climbing out of the vehicle, he said, "I know you've got somewhere you'd rather be tonight, and that's cool. Do whatever you want to do, and don't worry about me, Eric. I've got everything we collected, and I'll make sure it gets to Josh."

Anxious to get to Lydia and glad to see Chris more like himself, he smiled, and said, "Thanks to you, too. See you tomorrow."

16

Eric drove to Lydia's house and pulled into the drive-way. Her house was dark except for the porch light, which illuminated the front. Looking at his watch, he saw that it was two a.m., and he hesitated for a moment, pondering his options. He knew it would not be hard to pick her lock and enter quietly but wondered about explaining how a journalist would know how to pick a lock. Also, the idea of frightening her was not something he wanted to do. Nor, explaining his actions to the police, should she awaken and dial 9-1-1.

Deciding to take her at her word, he grabbed his phone and pressed the autodial for her number, which he had saved. It rang twice before she answered.

A mumbled "Eric?" was heard, and he was unable to keep the grin from his face. "Hey, babe. Is it too late?"

"Uh-uh. It's fine. You can come on over," she muttered.

"Good, because I'm already here." He got out of his

vehicle and walked up the steps. "Can you make it to the front door?"

"Uh-huh."

The phone line went dead, and he stood for a moment at her front door, uncertain if she had gone back to sleep or was actually making it down the hall. Finally, hearing the latch flip, he turned the knob and opened the door. The sight of a sleepy Lydia, wavy hair tousled about her head and dressed in pink pajama bottoms with a matching camisole, was exactly what he wanted to see.

The idea of what it might be like to come home to her every evening hit him like a punch to the gut. His breath left his lungs quickly, and he was glad that she had stepped forward and slid her arms around him, resting her head on his chest, because he was uncertain that he was able to move.

With her cheek against his heartbeat, he managed to slide his arms around her, encircling her protectively. He knew that she was mostly asleep, but even in that state she had moved instinctively into his arms. Before he gave too much thought about that, he kissed the top of her head, and said softly, "Come on, babe. Let's get you back to bed."

She mumbled something incoherent, and he felt her nod against his chest. Grinning, he turned her to face the hall, and with his arm wrapped around her shoulder, led her back to the bedroom. He had brought a change of clothing and as they entered the bedroom, he tossed his small bag to the side. Kissing the top of her head again, he said, "You get in bed, I'll be right there."

He stayed long enough to make sure that she actually made it to the bed before he walked into the bathroom. Quickly taking care of his business, he flipped off the light and padded over to the bed, peering down. Moonlight was coming through the slatted blinds, casting a slight illumination over her. Now her long waves were covering the pillow, and her face was relaxed in sleep. Lying on her side, her hands were tucked under her cheek as though in prayer. He stood, admiring her angelic pose, once again desiring to prolong their relationship beyond just the couple of days that were left.

Sighing at his wayward thoughts, he slid under the covers with her. Curving his body around her back, he tucked her tightly into his embrace. The scent of her shampoo filled his nostrils, already familiar. Closing his eyes, he memorized the feel of her in his arms, wanting to be able to take her with him when he left, in memory if not in reality.

As with most nights after a mission, he assumed he would find sleep eventually, but not right away. But tonight, with Lydia sleeping soundly in his arms, he closed his eyes and soon drifted away.

The next morning, Lydia stood in her driveway and kissed Eric, wanting nothing more than to grab his hand and run back inside. She had no memory of opening the front door to him in the wee hours, which caused her a certain amount of consternation, but waking up that morning feeling his warm heat against her back again made her wish for more mornings like that. Morning sex. A shared shower. Conversation and laughter over breakfast.

It had been hard when Caroline left, knowing that loneliness was going to become her constant companion. Caroline had even talked about wanting her to find someone special to share her life with. And now she had found someone that made her heart race...and it was only temporary.

Feeling Eric's arms squeeze around her, she shivered as his breath moved across her ear. "Whatcha thinking about?"

She looked up and smiled, shaking her head slightly. "I'm thinking how glad I am that you decided to come to me, even if I was a zombie in the middle of the night."

He laughed, and said, "I was glad you unlocked the door for me, but I have to say I'm a little concerned that you don't remember it at all. I can only hope that you wouldn't do that for someone else."

"Well, I hardly think that a robber is going to call me and ask for entrance," she quipped.

"You never know. You might end up with a polite robber who asks for permission to enter, and you grant it in the middle of the night and then not remember it."

She liked this...the easy banter. The fun. The laughter. It had been a long time ago, but she remembered this with Tim. She used to wonder, if he had lived, what life would have been like. Would they have stayed happy? She liked to think that they would have.

"Your mind is moving all over the place this morning," he said, peering closely at her.

Nodding, she knew it would be feckless to try to deny it. She leaned back and held his gaze, his eyes warm, but assessing. "I was just thinking how nice it is to have you here in the mornings. I know it's only been two mornings, but I've loved waking up with you. Please don't be embarrassed with me mentioning Tim, but I couldn't help but wonder how nice it would've been all these years to have had someone to wake up with." Giving her head a little shake, she continued, "I know that's not what we are. We're temporary, and I get that. But it's been nice with you. It's been good to spend time with someone that I truly like so very much."

His arms tightened once again, and his lips curved in a gentle smile. "I'm not embarrassed to think that I have any comparison to Tim. From all you've told me, he seemed like a very good man and a good husband to you. I'm sorry for his loss and that Caroline was never able to really know him. But I'm so impressed with what you've done for yourself. And," he bent to kiss the tip of her nose, "I've had the same kind of thoughts about you. Being with you the last couple of days has been unexpected and is very welcome. I wish...well, I suppose wishes don't really help at this point."

She sucked in a ragged breath and forced another smile on her lips. "I've got to get to work, so I'll drag my arms away from you so that you can leave, too."

He bent and took her lips in another kiss before stepping away. Just as he was about to get into his car, he said, "Don't forget about tonight. Reservation's at six."

She watched him drive down the road and sighed at how short his time was left in Kansas. *I knew what this was when I started it,* she chided, walking to her car. Pulling out of the driveway, her thoughts in a whirl, she knew that even with the sadness of having him leave, she had no regrets about opening her heart up to him.

Pain and heartache, as well as love and joy, often went hand-in-hand. *I'll take them all anytime over just being alone.*

Arriving at his hotel, Eric went to his room to drop off his bag, then, not seeing Chris, headed down the hall. Knocking, Chris called out for him to come in. Stepping into the room, he grinned at the sight of Chris sprawled on the sofa. He had been impressed to learn that Chris had set up surveillance so that he would know who was outside his door, but now he had to wonder if it was just so he would not have to get up to answer it.

Chris had a room that was identical to his, and he made his way over to the chair, taking the same position as they did in his own room. The anxiety from last night seemed to have left Chris, who greeted him with a wide smile.

"Got anything for me this morning?"

Nodding, Chris said, "Those guys at Lighthouse are freaking phenomenal. They must have gotten very little sleep, because they're already working on things this morning. The data we got is encrypted, but they're working through that and said they'd have no problem extrapolating the information. I told them that names were important, and we'd leave it up to DHS to decide what to do with it—hell, they probably want to share it with the FBI, ATF, even the CIA. But, I also told them what we were most interested in was any financial records that could be tied into activities against the facility here."

Impressed, he grinned. "Good job, man."

"And, that's not all."

Eric lifted an eyebrow. "My, my, you've been busy this morning."

"Yeah, but not having as much fun as I'm sure you did this morning."

"Careful there," he warned, not wanting Lydia to be part of any banter.

Throwing his hands up in defense, Chris said, "Oh, no offense intended. She seems real nice, and I'm glad you got somebody in your life."

A wrinkle appeared in his forehead, and he admitted, "She's in my life for now, but we both know it can't go anywhere else."

Chris' head jerked back, startled, and he asked, "Why the hell not? If you two like each other and seem to get along great, what's the problem?"

"I don't live here. I live halfway across the country."

"People do long-distance all the time. You've got frequent flyer miles, time to travel, email, Skyping—"

Throwing his hands up, he replied, "I know, I get you. I just don't think that's for me." Thinking about how Lydia commented how much it meant to her to wake up to him, and how many years she had gone without that kind of closeness, he added, "I don't think that's fair to either one of us. That kind of relationship is hard."

Chris was silent for a moment, before adding softly, "Well, at least if you really like her, then you two can be friends."

A sudden pain hit him right in the upper left side of his chest. Friends. *Would that be enough? For her? Hell, would it be enough for me?* Uncertain of the answer, he shook his head, refocusing on the task at hand.

Standing, he said, "I'm heading back over to the NBAF for the final day of the conference. This will be my last day to observe the journalists. I need you to work with Josh and Clay today, and try to come up with some kind of a connection that ties up all the loose ends we're looking at. So far, right now, all I've got are two protesting groups that I've learned very little about beyond the information I was given before I came. I also know that I have my suspicions concerning the Chinese, Russian, and one of the South Korean journalists, but I have no evidence beyond my own instinct. Which means, so far on this mission, I've got a big, fat, fuckin' nothing."

"Don't worry, man. You go see what else you can find out and I'll keep digging on this end."

With a nod, he pushed himself up from the chair and walked out of Chris' room. Heading out of the hotel to his car, his thoughts wandered once more to his last days with Lydia. Pulling out his phone, he double checked the reservation, and a slight smile crossed his face at the thought of their evening together.

17

Sitting near the back of the room afforded Eric the opportunity to observe all the players in the various scenarios acting out in front of him. Seo-yun appeared blissfully ignorant of her partner, Ji-Ho, as he sat next to Chang. While Egor seemed interested in Ji-Ho the other day, it appeared today he was firmly stuck to the Russian scientist who had come to the conference.

In fact, with the exception of Ji-Ho and Chang, it appeared that all of the journalists were sitting with the scientist from their respective countries. After the morning break, he moved closer, unnoticed by the others, until he was almost directly behind Chang and Ji-Ho.

Today was the last day and, so far, there had been no inkling of a disruption to the NBAF. He wondered if the chatter that Silas and Paul had referred to was nothing more than false information and, therefore, his mission a feckless exercise. *Other than meeting Lydia.*

The afternoon hours seemed to move even more slowly as the conference was winding down. Just when Dr. Hughley began her final presentation on African Swine Fever, he felt a vibration in his pocket. His keychain had been fitted with a small transmitter that allowed Chris to let him know that he was needed.

Standing, he left the auditorium and moved to the front of the building. Checking out with the guard, he commented, "Got plans to quit smoking, but it's not happening right now." The guard waved him on, and he headed out to the parking lot. Grabbing his phone, he dialed Chris. "What have you got?"

"Still working with Josh and Clay, but they've already come up with some interesting information. I'm really calling because Mace wanted to talk to you."

"They're finishing the lectures right now, so I'll talk to Mace then go back in for my final look at everyone. After that, I'll be back to the hotel. You can brief me before I take Lydia out this evening."

"You got it, boss."

Disconnecting with Chris, he called Mace. "What have you got?"

"We've already run the fingerprints through all national databases and have a hit."

Surprised at how quick Mace was able to get that accomplished, he waited to hear what he would say.

"I can see why the person who talked to you used a blindfold and a voice changer. Your John Doe is Robert Edger. He's been arrested several times for petty vandalism but in recent years has stepped it up. He has an outstanding warrant in an arson case concerning a dog food manufacturing company. The FLA claimed that putting real meat in dog food should be illegal, so they attempted to bomb the factory."

Analyzing the information, he bit out, "So now he's here in Kansas, getting ready to do whatever the fuck he wants to do with the NBAF?"

"I know that your team member has been working with my guys, but so far they haven't been able to pull anything out of the computer. It almost looks like it's been wiped clean. My guys are digging deeper to make sure that's not just a cover. My guess is that when Robert left that building, he left the computer there as a diversion."

"And he didn't think to completely wipe down the desk?"

"May have been in a rush," Mace surmised. "Or maybe he thought someone else did it. Hell, maybe he did it himself and just didn't do a good enough job."

"Okay, Mace. You definitely get a marker for me on this. I'll take this information and start running with it." Disconnecting, he stood at his car for a moment, then placed a call to Chris.

"Mace's people have discovered the man I talked to was Robert Edger. His prints were the ones that I pulled up last night."

"No shit!"

Trying to ignore Chris' enthusiasm, he said, "Just listen. I need everything you can get on him. I also want to know what connection you can find between him, the Foundation for Liberating Animals, and any money he may have gotten from foreign sources. I hate to put pressure on you, but I need this information ASAP, because if he left that building quickly, then he may know somebody's onto him, and that may cause him to escalate any plans."

"No worries, boss. I'm on it."

Disconnecting once again, he thought of the people inside. Heading back through the guard gate, he slipped inside the auditorium for the last part of the conference. Once again sitting near the back, he wondered if it would be possible to get the fingerprints from the other Asian male journalists. Noting where Zhang, Wang, and Ji-Ho were sitting, he watched carefully to see where they placed their hands.

Finally, the last of the questions were answered and Dr. Hughley, Paul, and several of the other NBAF bigwigs thanked the scientist and journalists for their interest in disease prevention.

Moving quickly to the side, he watched as Ji-Ho and Zhang put their papers into briefcases, and both men placed their hands on the back of the seat as they pushed themselves to a standing position. His eyes darted over to Wang and noted that he put his hands flat on the arms of the auditorium seat as he stood.

Everyone began filing out of the room slowly, chatting as they said goodbye to each other. The Russians left first, followed by the Chinese. After a few more minutes of goodbyes with the rest of them, they all left the room, heading back to the front of the building to leave.

Knowing time was of the essence, he jerked his head to the side at Paul, who was still standing on the stage with several of the other presenters. Giving a short nod, Paul ushered them off the stage and out of the room.

With the small auditorium now empty, he rushed to Wang's seat and, using his fingerprint tape, lifted prints from where Wang's hands had been. Marking those, he shoved them into his briefcase before moving to Zhang's chair and doing the same.

Just as he got to Ji-Ho's seat, he heard a noise and looked up as Paul walked back in, moving directly to him.

"You got something?"

"Possibly. I needed everyone out to grab some fingerprints."

With a nod, Paul said, "Thank you. I know we made it through the seminar without any incidents, so I realize this may have been all for naught. But, take what you need, because something may still come out of this." With that, Paul left the auditorium, leaving Eric to finish his job.

Taking prints from Ji-Ho's chair, he slid those tapes into his briefcase as well. With one last look around, he walked out of the room. The last of the scientists and journalists were still at the guard counter, going through the process of checking out. Before moving to join them, he looked behind him, knowing that in the back of the building, probably walking among pigs, was Lydia. A woman he never expected to meet. And now, a woman that he could not imagine not being in his life.

"Hi, Mom."

"Caroline, baby! How are you?" Unable to keep from grinning widely, Lydia moved out of the bathroom and sat on the edge of her bed.

"I'm fine. I had a late afternoon biology lab, and I'm walking back to the dorm, so I thought I'd give you a call."

"I'm glad you did. I've wanted to call you, but also wanted to make sure I let you get settled in without me hovering."

"Mom, you never hover. You can call me anytime you want, you know."

"I know you sent your schedule to me, but I don't know when you might have study groups or are out with friends. I'll probably keep doing what I've been doing, which is just text, and then you can give me a call when you're free."

"That'll work," Caroline said easily. "So how are you doing since I've been gone?"

"Missing you like crazy. I've learned firsthand that empty nest is real. But, I'm so glad you're having a good time. Do you think you might get a chance to see your grandparents sometime soon?"

"Actually, Mom, that's one of the reasons I was calling. I talked to Grandma yesterday and she wanted to know if we wanted to have Thanksgiving at their place, and you fly in. If your work schedule doesn't allow it, then Grandma and Grandpa and I will fly to Kansas so that we can all be together."

"I haven't even begun to look at the holiday schedule, but I think I can probably get off. What would you rather do? Spend it in Pennsylvania or come to Kansas?" She heard the hesitation, and said, "Honey, there's no right or wrong answer to this. It doesn't matter to me which table we're at, as long as we're all together for the holidays. I know that one day we won't all be together, so I cherish each one that we can."

Caroline sighed, and said, "I'd really like to come to Kansas, and I could see some of my friends from high school. I just don't know that Grandpa would enjoy flying."

"You're right, he probably wouldn't. Tell you what, how about if we do Thanksgiving on the East Coast and then you can do Christmas here in Kansas."

"Perfect," Caroline agreed. "So, what's new with you, Mom?"

She wondered if she should say anything, but then blurted, "I'm getting ready to go on a date tonight—"

"A date! Oh, my God, Mom! A date!" Caroline repeated, her voice full of youthful exuberance.

Laughing, she said, "Now don't get excited. It's with a man that I met here through a conference, and he'll be leaving to go back home soon."

"So, it's just a casual work thing?"

She hesitated a few seconds too long, and Caroline jumped back in.

"Mom? What's going on? Why do I get the feeling that this isn't just a casual work thing?"

"It's…complicated," she replied, wondering how much to tell her daughter. "It's nothing that's going to last, but I have to admit I really like him. So, if nothing else, it's made me realize that I still have a life to live."

Caroline's voice softened. "Mom, I'm so glad. I mean, I hope your heart isn't getting too involved considering that he's going to be leaving soon. But I always felt like you were holding back because of me."

Caroline's voice sounded more mature, leaving her in wonder at her daughter. "No, baby, that's not true. I held back because of me. I wanted to be there for you, and I wasn't willing to bring someone else into our lives unless I was sure. That may have been too cautious of me, but I have no regrets."

"Okay, okay," Caroline acquiesced. "So, tell me what you're wearing?"

Laughing, she replied, "I'm pulling out that wrap dress that you so like. The red one with the little ruffled sleeves."

"Oooh, I love that one!"

"Well, it's been hanging in my closet for a long time, and I finally decided it was time to wear it. I don't know what tonight will bring, but it feels like a little-red-dress kind of night."

They continued to chat and laugh for a few more minutes, before Caroline said that she was back at her dorm. Wishing her well and giving her love, they disconnected.

Her heart was trapped between a mix of heaviness and excitement, both for her daughter and, now, for herself. Glancing at the clock on her nightstand, she realized that they had been talking for fifteen minutes, and Eric would soon be showing at her door. Jumping up, she hurried into the bathroom to finish getting ready.

Looking into the mirror, she sucked in a deep breath and let it out slowly. Thinking back to the words she just told her daughter, she knew they were true. She still had a life to live.

18

Lydia's eyes were dancing with delight as she walked into Harry's in the old, downtown Wareham building. "I can't believe you got reservations here. How did you know this was the nicest place in Manhattan to eat?"

"I asked the receptionist at the hotel where I'm staying. I told her I was escorting a beautiful woman to dinner, and I wanted to take her to the nicest place in town. She said, no doubt, it would be Harry's."

She looked around, the interior familiar although she had only eaten here a few times. "I brought Caroline here a few months ago, just before she left for college. I always thought it was one of the prettiest restaurants I've ever seen."

The bar was behind a partial wall of dark, warm wood topped with elegant glass panels, each with an etched W in the middle. The highly polished wood and dim lighting cast a warm glow over the inviting interior. The tile floor, cream with black squares in the middle of each tile, paired beautifully with the buttery cream wood wainscoting and dark wallpaper. Each table was covered with a cream cloth and surrounded by comfortable, padded chairs.

With his hand resting on her lower back, she felt the tingles from Eric's fingertips straight through her whole body. Twisting her head around, she met his eyes and smiled before moving to follow the hostess to their table. Delighted to see that they had a private corner table, she settled into her seat, pleased that he sat next to her and not across. It made for more intimate seating but also allowed him to have a nice view of the beautiful surroundings.

After listening to the wine choices, they both selected and began to look over the menu. "Harry's is famous for their steaks."

He chuckled. "In the middle of Kansas, I would expect no less."

"Well, lots of places claim to have local beef, but whatever Harry's does to theirs, its magic in your mouth."

That comment sent his heated gaze toward her and a blush rising over her cheeks. "Oh, stop it," she chided, unable to hide her grin. "You know what I mean."

"I do know what you mean, but I also know what I'd like to do with the magic in your mouth as well."

Determined to move the conversation off of something that made her want to grab his hand and run out of the restaurant before they had eaten, she said, "Harry's is named for Harry Wareham, an integral member of Manhattan's history. In the early 1900s, he wanted to provide conveniences to the citizens here. He established a sewer system, a telephone system, and even brought the theater to town, providing the Wareham Theater. He also established an ice company and a lovely hotel, located above the restaurant. It's been turned into apartments, though."

Eyebrows raised, he said, "He sounds like a very industrious man."

"Kansas State University was founded in 1863, and as an original agriculture college, it was of course built in the middle of an agricultural area, which was not very populated. Kansas had only been admitted to the United States in 1861, so it was very new. I think by the time Harry came along in the late 1800s, early 1900s, he recognized that Manhattan was going to continue to be a thriving city. He was smart enough to recognize what businesses would need to be established to make a difference here in the quality of life and would make others want to come here as well."

"Are you a history buff?" he asked, smiling.

Shaking her head, she said, "I've lived in several places, and for some reason I've always desired to know the history of where I was living. Somehow it made it seem more real...more like home."

The server came by, and they ordered their dinner, then looked at each other over the candlelight. Her smile was sincere when she said, "Thank you for bringing me here tonight."

He leaned over and placed a chaste kiss on her lips. "I should be the one thanking you for the honor of your presence."

Blushing again, this time for an entirely different reason, she looked down at her wine glass before taking a sip. They sat quietly for a moment, and she took another sip of wine. Gaining her courage, she lifted her gaze back to his, and said, "Eric, I know what this is. And I don't want you to tell me anything you don't feel comfortable saying, and I certainly don't want you to make something up. But I feel like you know so much about me and, yet, there's so little I know about you."

Her words hung between them, and she wondered if he was going to give her an answer. Just when she wished their dinner would be served so that she could lose herself in the food, he spoke.

"I was once married."

As soon as the words left his mouth, Eric wished that he could pull them back in. The wide-eyed expression on Lydia's face gave him pause.

She must have realized that he was now uncertain, because she said, "Please, continue. I hope you feel free to tell me anything."

Breathing easier, he nodded. "I'm afraid my story isn't like yours and Tim's. I got married after college, but it didn't last very long. She was unhappy with my job, the amount of travel I had to do, and it wasn't nearly as exciting as she thought it was going to be."

Her brow furrowed, and she tilted her head slightly in question. "What did she think a journalist would be doing?"

Pondering his answer carefully, he said, "I wasn't a journalist then. I actually was in the military. She thought being married to someone in the service was going to be exciting. I have no idea where she got that idea, but staying home when I was deployed was not what she wanted it to be." Shrugging, he said, "In hindsight, I should've realized she was never cut out for that life. It's embarrassing to say that we met at a bar near a Navy base, where unfortunately many women troll to either bag someone for the night, or they're husband hunting, desperate to get out of whatever little town the base may be in. Looking back, I think she did love me, but not enough to accept me for who I was. When I would come home from being deployed, she was angry, and it didn't take long for me to realize that marrying her was a mistake. Quite frankly, she realized it first. We had only been married for a little over two years when she asked for a divorce."

She reached over and placed her hand on his, giving a little squeeze. "I'm so sorry you had to go through that. Did you ever remarry…or think of remarrying?"

Shaking his head, he replied, "No. I've dated but never for very long. I think I was a little relationship shy and, while I was in the military, it just did not seem like there was any point to trying again. I mean, I'm not opposed to marrying again, but it would need to be with someone really special, not just because I didn't want to be alone."

"And children?"

Shaking his head, a sigh left his lips. "We never had any, and I'm glad. It would have been hard, both with all my deployments and the divorce." Lifting his shoulders in a slight shrug, he added, "I do sometimes think about what I missed out on, and that includes children and grandchildren."

She reached across and held his hand tightly, her face etched in sadness. "I know it was a long time ago, actually for both of us, but I am sorry that your marriage was not a good one. I grieved and, in some ways, still grieve the loss of Tim, but it's with the knowledge that I had found a good man and we were happy."

"What about you?" he asked, linking his fingers with hers. "Did you never consider marrying again?"

Her lips curved slightly, as she said, "It's not that I was against having another relationship or marrying, but my first priority was always to Caroline. She was so young when he died, that between working, going to school, and taking care of her, there was no room for anything else. And regardless of how many people get married right away and have blended families, I was always so cautious. I didn't want to bring someone into Caroline's life who would come and go. I didn't want to bring someone into her life who wanted me, but just sort of accepted the fact that I had a child. Could I have found someone who would've loved us both? Who would've wanted to have raised her and loved her as their own?" Nodding, she answered her own questions when she said, "Yes. I'm sure there was someone out there, but I just never looked hard enough. We were happy together, and I knew that one day, when she was an adult, then something might happen for me."

He gave her hand a squeeze, and they sat quietly for another moment, sipping their wine. She looked over at him, and said, "Leaving the topic of our past relationships behind, I'm curious. How did you go from being in the military to becoming a journalist?"

He tensed slightly, deciding how honest to be. Maintaining a cover on a mission had never been a problem for him. He knew what he needed to say and how he needed to say it to convince a listener that he was exactly who he said he was. But now, sitting in the elegant restaurant with Lydia staring so intently at him, he swallowed deeply. Having no choice, he plunged ahead, but determined to give her as few lies as possible.

"I was in the service for twenty-five years and had to retire due to an injury. Too many jumps, and the knee just isn't the same as it was when I was a younger man." Chuckling ruefully, he added, "Probably that's true for the rest of me, as well."

A giggle snort erupted, and she said, "I've got no complaints with the rest of your body."

Laughing, he squeezed her hand, her words a balm to him. "At that time, I was just looking for a job. Being a journalist is the one that happened to land in my lap. I had a security clearance, so I was given this assignment."

She smiled and nodded, and he let out his held breath slowly.

"I understand that. As I told you, I went through

several jobs and levels of schooling to get to where I am now. I sometimes look at the young people in college now and wonder if they have any idea how many times their lives and careers will change as they get older."

He chuckled, both in relief of her acceptance of his explanation and in understanding of her statement. "You're so right. I've worked with some younger people whose enthusiasm is so intent on the job at hand, which is good and, yet, I wonder how long it will last."

"I always wanted Caroline to follow her dreams, but she watched me struggle through the years. As her mom, I tried to shield her from some of the harshness, but as a fellow woman, I wanted her to know that it's okay for us to not have all the answers all the time."

Just then, the server brought their steaks, and they turned their attention to the meal. He cut a bite of his filet mignon and groaned in ecstasy. Chewing the delectable morsel before swallowing, he looked over and saw her grinning widely at him. Not used to blushing, he could feel the heat on his face and laughed. "I can't help it. That was the most orgasmic bite of food I've ever had."

She snorted in laughter, then covered her face and blushed just as deeply as he was. "I swear, that sounds like something I would say." She took a bite of her own and closed her eyes as she enjoyed the flavors of the perfectly seasoned and cooked beef. After swallowing, she took a sip of wine, and then dared to look at him again. "Yes," she declared. "Definitely orgasmic."

They shared a laugh, and then went back to enjoying the rest of their meal. Deciding to forgo dessert, she asked, "How would you like to walk around the campus some? It's really beautiful, and I feel like I need to walk off some of my dinner."

Lifting her hand, he placed a kiss on her fingers, and replied, "That sounds perfect."

19

A few minutes later, Eric parked where Lydia directed, and they climbed from his vehicle. They walked along the sidewalks, the evening sun setting behind the buildings, painting the sky in royal colors. They watched the street lamps flicker on, illuminating their path.

As they walked along, she continued pointing out various sites. "When I first moved out here, I was amazed at the beauty of the Kansas prairies. It's nothing like where I was raised."

"Where was that?"

"I was raised in Pennsylvania. That was actually the Vet Med school that I went to, at the University of Pennsylvania. My parents still live in the eastern part of Pennsylvania, near Philadelphia. I didn't move here until I decided to do the internship. By then, Caroline was in high school and did not want to move again. So, I took the NBAF job so that she could graduate with her friends here."

"And Caroline now?"

Smiling widely, she answered, "She thought about going to Kansas State since she went to high school here, and I'm working here. But she really wanted to go back East, and since my parents are not too far away, I thought it was a good decision. She's also at the University of Pennsylvania."

They continued walking, their hands linked, and the thought crossed her mind that they looked like a real couple. It felt like being part of a real couple.

Before she had time to let her mind wander too far down that path, he asked, "Do you see yourself staying here? In Kansas?"

They stopped at a bench underneath tall trees with several streetlights around. Sitting down, she snuggled into his side as he wrapped his arm around her. "I've given that a lot of thought lately with Caroline gone. The NBAF has been good for me and good to me. The money has allowed me to pay off my student loans, the health insurance is excellent, and it's a secure job."

He looked down and pulled her closer, staring into her eyes. "I feel a *but* coming at the end of your statement."

She chuckled, and said, "You'd be right. It's not that I feel like I have to be where Caroline is. For all I know, she could move anywhere in the world when she graduates from college. Kansas is beautiful, and I've loved it here, but I don't feel like this is my forever place. I know my parents will be getting older, and I'd like to enjoy being around them more. Or, at least not halfway across the country from them."

"So, you think you might want to move back East sometime?"

"I think so. I haven't made any definite plans, but I'm certain it's where I'll end up."

"And pigs?"

Bursting out in laughter, she said through her giggles, "I don't feel like pigs are the only animals that I can take care of. I can certainly be a large animal vet, but I was also trained in small animals, so I could work almost anywhere." Grinning slyly, she added, "But, I might have to get a pig for a pet."

This time he chuckled, joining her laughter.

"How do you do that?" she asked, twisting her body to stare up at him.

His brow scrunched down, and he asked, "Do what?"

"Always find things out about me. Somehow it seems as though I end up blabbing all kinds of things about me. So, what about you? Where are you from?"

"Born and raised in North Carolina. I'm an only child. My parents were older when they had me. I never heard them discuss it, but I got the feeling that they had trouble getting pregnant and when I came along, I think they were rather surprised. Happy, but surprised."

"Are they still living?"

Shaking his head, he said, "No, my dad passed about ten years ago and my mom almost five years ago."

Taking both of his hands in her own, she held them tightly. "Oh, Eric, I'm so sorry. Here I've been talking about my family, not even thinking that you might have lost yours."

"Don't take that on, babe. I'm fine, really. I had a

177

wonderful childhood and my parents were very proud of me being in the military. Both of them passed away rather quickly, without a long, drawn-out illness. It's not like I don't have anyone in my life. Believe me, when you're in the military, your team is truly your band of brothers."

"I'm glad for you, that you have that." She twisted back around and settled into the crook of his shoulder, reveling in the feel of his arms around her. They sat for several minutes in silence, watching students rushing along the sidewalks as the young often do, always in a hurry.

Her voice slightly wistful, she said, "I know I'm not old, not in years. But sometimes I feel very old in experience. I look at these young people, whose lives lay out before them, and would not wish to be back where they are for anything. Everything I've gone through in my life, the good and the bad, the joy and the grief, has led me to where I am right now."

Eric stood and, with his hand in hers, gently pulled so that their bodies were aligned, face to face. Holding her gaze, he asked, "And are you happy with where you are right now?"

Her chest felt heavy, as though a weight were pressing her down, and she said, "Yes. I know you're leaving. I've known since the beginning that this was only temporary. And right now, my heart hurts knowing that our time together is almost over." She felt his arms band tighter around her and she continued, "But I wouldn't change one moment. Meeting you, spending time with you, has made me happier than I've been in a long time. Maybe, if nothing more, you've shown me that there's more out there for me. I'm not done with living."

He swooped down, claiming her lips in a kiss that stole her breath. His hands slid up to cup her jaw, holding her in place as he delved inside her warm mouth, stealing her essence. She gave as good as she accepted, wanting to press every second into her memory like a flower between the pages of a book. Knowing that, when he left, she could pull her memories out and feel just like she was feeling at this moment.

Finally, he leaned back, sucking in a ragged breath. She was panting as though at the end of a race, staring up at his face. He seemed to be battling with something, so she remained quiet, giving him the space he needed.

He dropped his chin and offered her a small smile. "I don't know how I'm going to say goodbye tomorrow," he admitted. "But I want to take you home right now so that I can have this one last night."

Arriving back at her house, they had barely made it through the door before he kicked it shut and whirled around, backing her against the wall. Hot and wild, they tore at their clothes, both desperate for skin to skin contact. Their noses bumped as their heads moved back and forth, a tangle of lips and tongues with kisses that branded.

Eric's heated kisses stopped as he bent to grab a condom. The cool air beaded Lydia's nipples and she was uncertain how she had become completely undressed so quickly, but a quick look around her showed her dress, bra, panties, and shoes lying all about the floor.

Chest heaving, she stared at his muscular, tight body, once again admiring his perfect male form. Young and adventurous, sex with Tim had been fun. But as Eric lifted her against the wall and impaled his erect cock deep inside her as she wrapped her legs around his waist, she was experiencing something new. Wall sex was something for romance novels, but she had never thought to experience it herself.

He pressed her back against the wall, helping to hold her in place with his forearms, which left her legs spread wide. The sensation was completely different as he thrust continuously, reaching deep inside her sex. He bent his head and pulled her nipple into his mouth, eliciting tingles that shot between her breasts and her core. Her legs began to ache slightly, but the pain was balanced with the tightening inside, her orgasm close.

"Touch yourself," he ordered, his voice gravelly with need.

She shifted one of her hands between their bodies and found her swollen nub. Pinching it slightly just as he increased his thrusts, she cried out as her orgasm rushed over her. Throwing her head backward, she hit the wall, but ignored that pain as well. As her body slowly stopped pulsating, she dropped her chin and held his gaze.

She watched as his jaw clenched, and the muscles in his neck stood out. Fascinated, she continued to stare as he finally threw his head back and roared, continuing to plunge. His movements slowed, and he lowered his chin, staring into her eyes for a moment, before he dropped his forehead to the wall just over her shoulder.

She wrapped her arms tightly around his neck and pressed their bodies together. No words were spoken. No words were needed.

He slowly pulled out and lowered her feet to the floor, continuing to support her body as the tingles began to cease in her legs. Once she was sure she was steady, she smiled up at him and watched his handsome face transform as he smiled back.

"God, please tell me I didn't hurt you," he said. "I was so rough—"

She shushed him with her fingers over his lips and shook her head. "Don't you dare apologize for what we just did. It was wonderful. Hell, it was more than wonderful. It was fuckin' fantastic."

He laughed, and she loved seeing his face full of amusement. As his mirth ended, he kissed her lightly, mumbling, "If we've only got one night, let's make it last."

She nodded her agreement, and they walked back to her bedroom, leaving their clothes scattered by the front door. Once in bed, they lay tangled in each other. The next time, it was not just sex. They made love with kisses, and murmurs, and words whispered in the dark as their bodies joined together.

20

Prolonging their goodbye for as long as possible, Eric and Lydia stood on her front porch. With his arms wrapped around her, he pressed her cheek against his chest and rested his against the top of her head. The scent of her floral shampoo, now so familiar, filled his nostrils.

She tilted her head back, her gaze holding his, and said, "I promised myself that this would be okay. I promised myself that I wouldn't cry, I'd give you a kiss and wish you well, and send you on your way."

He saw tears gathering in her eyes and the telltale sign of her chin quivering. "How are you doing with those promises?"

Her voice cracked as she replied, "Not very well." She blinked, and a tear slid down her cheek.

He swept his thumb across her petal soft skin and wiped the tear away, then leaned down to kiss the watery trail as another tear slipped down. "Just so you know, I made no such promises to myself, because I knew I wouldn't be able to keep them."

She swallowed audibly and inhaled a ragged breath deep into her lungs before letting it out in a long, slow sigh. "If you're ever back in this area...or, um...if you ever just want to chat..." She tightened her lips and gave her head a little shake, before blurting, "Sorry. I know that's not what this is—"

"I'd love to see you again." He rushed the words, wanting to get the sentiment out.

She stared up at his face, blinking adorably, as though uncertain of his words. "You do?"

"Absolutely. Lydia, we started out as just two adults having a good time. What we've ended up with, at least to me and I think to you, is a whole lot more. I haven't really thought this through, so I don't have any idea what I'm suggesting, other than, if nothing else, I'd like us to stay in touch."

A smile lit up her face, and he felt the punch straight to his heart. She nodded enthusiastically, and said, "I know I have very little experience in these things, but I know what I feel, and I feel the same way you do."

Sensing there was something more, he asked, "What else are you thinking?"

"Well, I was talking to Caroline, and I'll be flying to Pennsylvania for Thanksgiving. Maybe I could plan on seeing you sometime then."

He swooped in and took her lips in a celebratory kiss, knowing it was not the final kiss they would ever share. Memorizing every nuance of her mouth, he finally leaned up and placed a barely-there kiss on the tip of her nose. Giving her body a squeeze, he stepped back and said, "I've got a few things to take care of today, then my flight leaves this evening. I'll give you a call once I get to Kansas City. "

She nodded enthusiastically, and said, "That would be perfect. In fact, you can call me anytime." Heaving another sigh, she dropped her arms as well and stepped back.

He jogged to his vehicle and climbed in, tossing another wave her way before pulling out of her driveway. He had no idea what he was doing or how to make any of this work. All he knew was he was not ready to give up having her in his life.

"What have you got on Robert Edger?" Eric asked as Chris answered his call. He was on his way to the NBAF to tie up loose ends but wanted to see if Chris had made any break-throughs before he arrived.

"Probably some of the same stuff that you got from Mace. Messed up childhood with a dad that was arrested a couple of times for domestic violence. Mom finally took he and his siblings and moved out. Robert had a few skirmishes with the law as a teenager. I got into his closed files, and it looks like mostly just fights and vandalism. Does look like he got into a gang, not a major one, more like one where they did stupid shit... robberies with pretend guns, vandalism of school property, busting out windows in some businesses. A few more arrests that resulted in jail time but no serious prison time."

"Sounds like someone who's always searching for a group to belong to. At least that's my armchair psychology version."

Chris chuckled. "Yeah, I thought the same."

"Where's his official location?"

"He doesn't own any property. He was raised in Georgia and has rented apartments in South Carolina, Texas, and most recently had a warrant out for his arrest for arson in California."

Scrubbing his hand over his face, he said, "I'm heading back over to the NBAF to talk to Paul. Keep digging for a connection between Robert and any money trail."

"I've already gotten into his bank account and am just starting to see what I can find. I'll tell you, for a man who has no apparent employment, he's got money."

Pulling into the NBAF parking lot, he grinned. "Thank fuck. That might just be the link we're looking for."

Hanging up, he parked his vehicle and got out. He had already called Paul and was allowed easy access back into the building. As he walked down the hall, Paul met him, his hand out ready for a shake.

"I take it by you wanting this meeting, you've got something. Let's go into my office," Paul invited.

Walking in, he saw two other DHS employees waiting. After introductions, they sat down, and he quickly gave his information. "Robert Edger is the name of the person who is working locally with, or for, the FLA.

He's the one that granted me the interview that I've already told you about. My guy has already looked up his information and is currently checking out his finances. My guess? He's getting paid by a foreign source that wants to disrupt the NBAF."

Paul looked over at the two people in his office, and said, "Take care of this. Work on a warrant for Robert Edger. Get that location from Eric, and I want a search warrant as well."

He gave them the information that he had and watched as the two others walked out. Paul spoke, turning his attention back to him.

"Do you think that's it? Do you think that all the chatter was just about Robert Edger and it didn't have anything to do with any of the foreign journalists that were here?"

Shaking his head, he said, "My gut says there's something up with Ji-Ho. He cozied up at one time to Egor from Russia, but I didn't get a feeling about them. He also spent time with the two journalists from China. That was a little harder for me to get a read on. But what really got my spidey senses going, was when he was pressuring Dr. Hughes on the levels of security for the researchers with security clearances."

Seeing Paul's eyebrows raised, he added, "She didn't give him any information, of course, and Ji-Ho moved away when I elbowed my way in."

"I've got a rush on the fingerprints that you took. Once they're in, we'll run them through our foreign databases to see if there are any differences with the passports they came in on."

Knowing that Mace had been able to get that information quickly, he rubbed his chin, and asked, "When do you think you'll have those?"

Grinning, Paul said, "You think DHS can't get it quick? Don't worry, we should have them by this afternoon."

Nodding, he pushed out of his chair and shook Paul's hand. "My flight doesn't leave until this evening, so I'll be around for a few more hours. I went ahead and paid the hotel rooms through today, so my team member and I will be there continuing to look at the finances for Robert Edger. If you need me for anything you can get hold of me."

"It's been good to work with you, Eric. I'll let you know what we find."

Arriving back at the hotel, he found Chris busy at work. Tossing his bag to the side, he plopped down into the chair. "Anything yet?"

"Still working." Instead of looking back down at his computer, Chris held his gaze for a moment.

Noting Chris' hesitation, he asked, "What's on your mind? Never known you to ponder over something without blurting it out."

Chris chuckled and shook his head. "I was just kind of wondering about this mission. I mean, it's not like it was a bust. You did have a weird as shit meeting with someone that we now know is Robert Edger. We know that we can look for a connection between him and foreign money, especially as it pertains to the animal extremist group, but it seems like everything else was kind of a waste."

An image of Lydia flashed through his mind and the thought slammed into him, *You're wrong. Nothing about being in Kansas turned out to be a waste of time.* Instead of sharing that personal info, he said, "Look, not every mission is going to be exciting. I warned you that this was probably not going to be a going in guns–blazing kind of mission. I'm still waiting on the fingerprint reports, not convinced that Ji-Ho is an innocent journalist. But," throwing his hands out to the side, "we did what we said we were going to do. We were here during the foreign conference, and we gave DHS our information."

Nodding slowly, Chris said, "I know. You're right. I guess I was just hoping there might be something a little more exciting." His face brightened, and he smiled. "Although we did get to go sneaking into that building, so that was pretty cool."

Unable to keep a bark of laughter held in, he said, "I'm gonna go take a shower. You keep digging."

Rushing around, trying to finish getting ready for work, Lydia did not mind the hectic pace, considering she was late due to her extended morning with Eric. She had so dreaded the sunrise, knowing it was her goodbye with him, but with his admission that he wanted to continue seeing her, or at least be friends, she was walking on air.

"Hey, Jim? Sorry I'm late, but I'm getting ready to walk out of my house. I'll see you in about twenty minutes. Tell Beth that I'll take her extra reports this afternoon since she has to cover for me right now."

Running back into the kitchen to make sure her coffee maker was turned off, she glanced at the rinsed dishes sitting in the sink and smiled. Starting tomorrow, there would only be her dishes and not Eric's, but she reminded herself that it was not the end of the two of them.

She slipped on her shoes and reached for the doorknob as she turned back to grab her briefcase and purse. Her doorbell rang, startling her, and she pulled her hand back to grasp her chest. Taking a deep breath, she opened her door and observed a young man, his hair slightly longish but slicked over, wearing a dark brown suit. She did not recognize him, but she was already late and needed him gone.

"I'm afraid this isn't a good time," she began, "and there's nothing that I need—umph!"

He stepped over the threshold into her foyer, pushing her backward.

"Get out!" she screamed, reaching for her purse to get her phone. He was much larger than her and overpowered her quickly, in spite of her best efforts to fight back, pulling her back and slamming her against the wall.

In her struggle, the table next to the door crashed to the floor, and the contents of her purse spilled out. She continued to scream until he clamped his large hand over her mouth.

Growling, "Shut up, Doc," he threw her to the floor and held her down, straddling her body. Grabbing her wrists with one hand, he pinned them against her stomach and used a knee to keep them in place as he pulled a syringe out of his pocket.

With his other hand still over her mouth, she fought to breathe as the panic of seeing the syringe settled inside her chest. Wiggling as hard as she could, she tried to buck him off her, but it was useless. Pain pierced her upper arm, and she quickly quieted.

Her world grew fuzzy, and the last thought she had before the darkness overtook her, was of Caroline.

21

Eric and Chris spent the rest of the morning working in the hotel room, Chris' knee bouncing in excitement every time he found a new lead to follow.

"I've gotten into Robert's bank information and, like I said, for someone with no employment record at this time, he's getting money."

Eric stared at him and waited. Lifting his eyebrows, he prodded, "And...?"

"Oh yeah. It's definitely from an Asian bank... South Korea. Now, here's where it gets interesting. Up until recently, South Korea and North Korea did not share any financial institutions. But there was a recent summit in Singapore that involved the U.S. and North Korea. To get ready for that, the South Korean banks established inter-Korean financial business."

"So, what you're saying is that the money that went to Robert from a South Korean bank, could actually be from someone from North Korea."

Grinning, Chris flipped his pen up into the air and snatched it back, shouting, "Bingo! Give that man a prize!"

Rolling his eyes for what seemed like the millionth time since he had met Chris, he once again prodded, "And...?"

"The money came from an account in North Korea. The name on the account is Hyun-Gi Kwun."

"So, Hyun-Gi Kwun is sending Robert Edger money from North Korea, ostensibly to fund the FLA." Flipping open his phone, Eric called Paul. "We're still here in town, doing some more digging until we leave for Kansas City and my flight. Got more information I wanted to pass on. Robert Edger has been getting money from a North Korean source. Name is Hyun-Gi Kwun."

"Thanks, Eric. By the way, I was just going to call you. I know this might be a little presumptuous, but since you recently spent time in Dr. Hughes' lab, I wanted to let you know that her assistant just got hold of me. It seems she was running a little late but has not shown up for work yet. She called to let him know she would be here shortly, but that was over an hour ago."

The hairs on the back of his neck stood up, his spidey senses on alert, and he lept from his seat. He had learned over his many years as a SEAL to trust that instinct, and he was not about to second guess it now. "I'm on my way over to her house," he said, his voice tight with fear.

"I wasn't suggesting you do that, I just thought I'd let you—"

"Had no reason to say anything because it was no one's business, but I became involved with her since I got here. She means something to me, and your words are sending a sense of fear straight through me. I know where she lives, I'm on my way. I'll call you as soon as I find out something."

Turning, he found Chris had already slammed his laptop shut and was shoving it into his backpack. "I can handle this alone," Eric said.

Shaking his head, Chris replied, "No need. I'm here, so let's go do this."

With no reason to argue, he gave a terse nod of his head, and they rushed out to his car. "Drive separately in case we need to split up later. You can follow me."

He hoped Chris' driving skills were good because he was going to need them since Eric was driving like a bat out of hell to get to Lydia's house. Turning into her driveway, he was barely aware of Chris pulling in behind him as he spied Lydia's car still in the driveway, but her front door standing open.

Jumping from his vehicle, his feet pounded up her front walk, and he rushed through the door. At a quick glance, the table by the front door was tipped over, and her purse was several feet away with its contents scattered, including her cell phone. As his eyes dropped, his heart squeezed tightly. Two small drops of blood lay on the floor immediately in front of him.

He began to kneel, but Chris grabbed his shoulder. "Gloves," Chris said, handing rubber gloves to him.

Snapping them on, he said, "Get Paul. Tell them what we've got. Tell him to get a team here."

He carefully looked through the items on the floor, but they all appeared to be from Lydia and not her assailant. Standing, he placed his hands on his hips and forced his mind to visualize what may have happened. Her slim briefcase was still near the front door, so she must have been almost ready to leave, but had not stepped out with everything yet. Since her purse was toward the living room, it may have been in her hand or on the table and was knocked to the side, therefore scattering the contents. Her phone was in it, therefore she had no way to call for help now and they could not track her with the GPS.

And the blood? *Fuck!*

Chris stepped over. "Paul's on his way. He'll have a crew with him. I'm gonna run and see if any of her neighbors saw someone here."

Jerking his gaze up to Chris, he said, "Thanks, man. Good idea." As Chris left the house, his eyes dropped back to the blood. *It's not a lot, so she wasn't stabbed. It's not splattered, so it's not as though she was hit. Something scratched or pierced her skin enough to have it bleed just a little.*

He moved back to the front door and looked around. The pots of flowers that sat on her front steps were undisturbed. That gave evidence to there not being a struggle outside of her house.

Turning to look back inside, he analyzed what he had observed and drew one conclusion—*She was drugged. She struggled, fought back, and then was drugged. If somebody was fighting while having an injection jabbed into them, they would easily bleed a little. Whatever she was given must have taken the fight out of her, making it easier to get her out of here.*

Paul and his team arrived, immediately swarming the area. He quickly brought them up to speed on his observations and consusion.

"Why the fuck her?" Paul growled. "This makes no sense. She has a low-level security clearance. She's in animal care, not research. If this is the work of one of the protesting groups, it doesn't make any sense. Kidnapping her does not disrupt the function of the NBAF."

Shaking his head, he fought the gut churning feeling coursing through him. Chris came running back inside, and said, "Only one neighbor saw a car this morning. Said it was a dark SUV, and he saw a man in a brown suit get out. His dog was barking, and his wife yelled at him to deal with it, so he walked away from the window and didn't see anything else. The next time he looked out, the SUV was gone."

Paul turned to one of his agents and barked for him to get over to interview the neighbor. Chris looked at Eric, and said, "Whatever you need, man. Just name it."

Standing with his heart in his throat, he replied, "Thanks, but right now, I don't have a fuckin' clue."

A rocking motion bounced her slightly, but Lydia could not figure out where she was, even as her eyes blinked open. As she slowly regained consciousness, she found herself lying in the back seat of an automobile, her hands taped together in front of her. Reality slowly crept in, as the memory of the man at her front door and the sting of the injection came to mind.

As she continued to blink, her focus slowly cleared, and she could see the back of the man driving the vehicle. Shifting her gaze, she saw no one in the passenger seat. The rocking stopped, but she was too afraid to move, not wanting him to realize she was awake.

That plan was quickly irrelevant, as he jerked around in the seat and saw her staring at him. "Fuck, you're awake."

He climbed out of the driver's seat and walked around to the rear passenger door, throwing it open. He was obviously trying to avoid the possibility of her feet kicking out at him, since he came to where her head was resting on the seat. "Sorry, Doc. I gotta keep you out for a while."

She wanted to scream, but a gag had been tied around her mouth. She tried to look upward again, but before she could wiggle away, another piercing pain hit her arm. The heavy, weighted blanket of darkness descended once again and, this time, she wondered if she would ever awake.

The man glanced around him for a moment and then pulled out his phone. "I'm here, at the airport. I thought you said someone would meet me." He listened for a moment, and then said, "Where? Oh, yeah, I see it. When should we get to Denver?" Another pause. "Yeah, it fuckin' matters, I just had to knock her out again, and I want to know how long this one might last." Receiving an answer, he disconnected, shoving his phone back into his pocket.

He climbed back into the driver's seat and drove to the destination in his instructions. Seeing a small private hangar, he drove around to the side. Checking in with the pilot, he said, "You just do what you were paid to do and get us there. I'm going to get the passenger on board."

Going back to his SUV, he opened the back door once again. Hauling her out, he threw her over his shoulder, hefted her in place, and walked to the small plane. Climbing inside, he dumped her unceremoniously into the seat.

The pilot got into the cockpit and looked over his shoulder. "You gotta buckle her in."

Grumbling, Robert leaned over and snap the belts around her waist, including the shoulder straps. Her head dangled forward, and he pushed her forhead back and to the side, so that it was resting against the headrest. Settling into his seat, he buckled in and told the pilot, "Now get going. I have no idea how much of a head start I might have, and I want to get us to Denver as soon as possible."

———

Eric went back to Paul's office where the DHS was currently running their investigation, and paced, waiting for Chris to get there.

Paul had given permission for Chris to bring his computer into the facility. Eric looked up as his partner entered the room and walked his way. "You have everything?"

Chris answered, "Yep. We're all checked out from the hotel, and I've got everything we need right here. Have you heard anything yet?"

Eric shook his head in a jerky motion and was grateful when Chris just sat down, not saying anything else, and began working on his computer.

Paul got off the phone, and said, "Immigrations and Customs Enforcement are on the lookout for Ji-Ho, based purely on our wanting to question him. I've also got TSA on the lookout for Robert Edger."

For a man used to controlling his destiny, Eric found pacing Paul's office to be maddening. Over the next thirty minutes, several others came and went out of the room, either giving information to Paul or taking his orders.

Suddenly, a young woman popped her head in, and said, "A rental car registered to Robert Edger was just found at the Topeka airport."

Eric shared a look with Paul and read in his eyes that they were on the same page. *Robert is trying to get her out of Kansas.*

He wanted to rush from the building and get to the airport as soon as he could but knew that would be folly. If Robert was already in Topeka, then he probably had already taken a plane out of there. *But how the hell would he have gotten an unconscious Lydia on a plane?*

"Have someone look at all the private planes that have left within the last hour," Eric barked out. The young woman appeared startled, and her gaze shot between him and Paul.

"Just do it!" Paul ordered.

From the side of the room, Chris said, "I'm already on it, boss."

He shot him a grateful look and moved over to stand behind him. He was amazed at how fast Chris' fingers flew over his keyboard, moving from one site to another.

"Topeka must not be all that busy," Chris said. "Only six private planes have taken off so far today and only two of those within the last hour."

Paul, on the phone again, said to the person on the line, "Where did the last two private planes go and who were the passengers? And I want that information fuckin' yesterday!" He did not hang up and after less than a minute, finished with, "Check the cameras and send the shot to me."

In a moment, Paul was sitting back at his desk, staring at his computer. Eric had moved from behind Chris to standing next to Paul as they stared at the screen together. A man pulled up to a small aircraft and talked with the pilot for a minute before returning to his car and pulling an unconscious woman from the back. Slamming his hand on the desk, he cried out, "That's him. And, fuck, that's Lydia!"

Chris called out, "That plane is going to Denver."

Eric stood for a moment, his fists on his hips, his mind racing in a chaotic manner, so unlike him. He tried to think rationally but all he could see was Lydia's face. *She must be so scared.* Anger and panic warred with his instinct to analyze the situation.

He lifted his head and pinned Chris with his stare. "We gotta go."

Chris was already jumping up, gathering his computer, no questions asked, when Paul argued, "You can't go running all over the country. Stay and work the problem from here. I can get people at the various destinations to check on what's going on."

"Not going to happen, Paul. I may be one step behind them at each destination, but by God I'm going to be a lot closer than I am sitting right here. You keep running the show from here. I'm heading to Denver. Chris is going with me, and I've got some other people I can call in. Every bit of information I get, we'll give to you. I'd appreciate it if you do the same for me."

Paul held his gaze for a moment, then said, "Fine. I'll have someone drive you to the Manhattan Municipal Airport. It's small, but we keep an airplane there. I'll call ahead and have a pilot ready to get you to Denver."

He shook Paul's hand and was just turning to head out of the room, when Paul's assistant called out, "Sir, Silas Branson is on your secure line."

He halted in his steps and looked at Paul, who picked up his phone and hit speaker.

"Si? You're on speaker. I've got Eric Lopez here with me."

"Eric, Paul's been keeping me briefed, and that includes this morning. I just needed to let both of you know that we've intercepted some Asian chatter coming from North Korea. We are uncertain of the exact location it's coming from, but they indicated that Dr. Linda Hughley, the head of research at NBAF, was abducted."

The feeling of being punched in the gut hit him hard, but he stood rooted to the floor. His gaze shot from Paul to Chris and then back down to the speakerphone.

"Silas, Dr. Linda Hughley is fine," Paul explained. "I saw her when I first came in. Who they've taken is Dr. Lydia Hughes."

Eric looked up, wide-eyed, and they locked gazes. "Fuckin' hell! They've taken the wrong person."

22

Eric was on the phone while Chris drove them to the small, Manhattan, Kansas airport. He had a few calls to make, but Mace was first on his list. Before he was able to get a word out, Mace spoke.

"Eric, we're here for you. Chris talked to Josh and filled us in on what's going on. What do you need from us?"

"Chris' been doing a lot of background work, but right now he's with me, and we're going to be in the air soon. We're running into a roadblock with Robert Edger. We know he's getting money from Hyun-Gi Kwun, and it looks like it's coming from South Korea, but could actually originate from North Korea. We need that trail followed and we need to find out who the hell Kwun is. I know Robert isn't calling the shots. With the chatter coming from North Korea about the abduction, my bet is Hyun-Gi is in charge of whatever they're planning."

"Josh and Clay are working on the money trail, as well as Kwun. I also wanted to let you know that Rank is currently in Los Angeles, finishing up a job there. I've already been in contact with him and he wants to be in on this with you, if you want him."

Glad for the assistance, he replied, "Abso-fucking-lutely. Rank and I go way back."

"I know you two were SEALs together. I'll coordinate with him until you all meet up. You're on your way to Denver?"

"Yes, but don't have him meet us in Denver. I'm convinced whoever is behind this is going to try to get her out of the country. If they just wanted to disrupt the NBAF, then they could be anywhere, but I think someone wants Linda Hughley's expertise."

"And when they find out they don't have Linda Hughley, but Lydia instead?"

Mace had just put into words what he was refusing to think about. "I don't know. But as long as they keep moving, I've got to think that they don't know yet they've got the wrong person."

"I'll tell Rank to expect your call. He'll stay in Los Angeles until he hears from you," Mace agreed. "And I'll have Josh and Clay in contact with Chris. I've also taken the liberty of calling Jack Bryant, of the Saints. He's got an investigative team based out of Virginia. I know Bart Taggart, another one of your former SEAL team members, works for him. It just so happens that Bart is in Las Vegas for a second honeymoon. Rank made contact with Bart, and he's in as well."

"Fuck, Mace, you know I'll take all the help I can get,

especially from some of my former team members, but his second honeymoon? Jesus."

"I asked the same thing, but today was their last day, and they were going to fly out. Bart is putting his wife on the plane back to Virginia, then he's heading to Los Angeles to meet up with Rank. They'll be there together, waiting to hear from you."

"I can't thank you enough, Mace."

"No thanks needed and no markers owed. And Eric? You'll find her."

Disconnecting, he hoped Mace was right. Rubbing his hand over his face, he had one more call to make. "Preacher? It's Eric Lopez. I'm gonna need your help." As succinctly as possible, he explained the sitution to Logan Bishop. "Bart and Rank are going to meet up in Los Angeles and await my next instructions. You're a master at logistics. I'm gonna need a little help pulling all this together."

Receiving Logan's assurance that he was already mapping out the coordinates of everyone involved and that he would stay in contact with him, they disconnected. He fired off a message to Rank and Bart, letting them know that Logan was working with them as well.

Chris looked over as he finished typing the message, and said, "Sounds like we got a team, boss."

He nodded, uncertain that his voice would hold as he thought about his former SEAL team members willing to drop everything to help him, and their bosses who had their own businesses to run, giving their assistance as well.

Chris turned onto the road leading to the airport

and, looking at the small building, Eric said, "No wonder Paul keeps his own plane here. It's tiny as fuck and not much traffic."

"Yeah, I checked. It's all airline alliances." A guard waved them through the gate, and Chris drove to one of the small hangars off to the side. While he talked to the guard, Chris grabbed their belongings and hustled to the small plane.

He shook hands with the pilot, who told him, "Don't worry, I'll get you to Denver posthaste. Climb aboard and get buckled in. As soon as I get the signal, we're outta here."

True to his word, the pilot had them airborne within five minutes. As the plane gained altitude, Eric looked out the window, across the Kansas vista. The rolling hills, prairies, and huge ranches surrounding farmhouses all met his view. He remembered thinking how beautiful it was when he first arrived. And now, all he could think about was getting away from it and getting to Lydia. Closing his eyes for a moment, he vowed that the next time he came back to Kansas, it would be with her.

"It'll take us about three hours," the pilot called back. "The winds are favorable, so I'll see if I can shave some of that time off."

Chris looked over, and asked, "Tell me what you need, Eric."

He shook his head slowly, and admitted, "My brain is fuckin' mush right now. And that pisses me the hell off."

Leaning closer, Chris held his gaze. "When Silas first came to me with this assignment, he told me that he was picking the best. He said there was nobody better than a former SEAL Commander for this kind of mission. Fast analysis, the ability to pull together multi-agencies into a cohesive team... I know, right now, all you can think about is Lydia's safety. But Eric, you've got this. And you've got others who are going to be right here for you. I'll do anything you tell me to do, boss, but I'm gonna need you to let me know what that is."

Nodding slowly, he allowed Chris' words to settle deep inside. He was right. He needed to force his emotions to the side and focus on the problem. Sucking in a deep breath, he said, "Okay. I appreciate your vote of confidence."

Shifting around slightly, he said, "I've got two former SEAL team members who now work for security firms. One of them, Rank, works for Mace. He's a coworker of Josh and Clay, so they're bringing him up to scratch on everything we've got so far. The other one, Bart, works for another security firm, and he's meeting up with Rank. Those two men have worked together as SEALs under me, and the three of us worked a mission a few months ago when Rank's girlfriend was also kidnapped."

Chris' eyes widened, and his mouth dropped open. "Jesus, does that happen a lot to the women involved with you security types?"

His brow scrunched for a second as he thought, but then he just shrugged. "I have no idea, but I'm not taking the fuckin' time to call them all up and asked them."

Blinking, Chris blushed from his neck right up to his red hair. "Sorry, boss," he mumbled.

For a brief second, he smiled, Chris' personality once more bringing a moment of mirth to the situation. "Rank and Bart are going to meet in Los Angeles and await my instructions. Paul already has someone in Denver checking into the flights going and coming. Because they have about a four-hour head start, chances are they may have already left Denver. By the time we get there, we should know what the deal is. As soon as we find out their next leg, we'll get hold of Rank and Bart and they'll meet us."

Nodding, Chris said, "Okay. Got it. Once we get to Denver, while you're finding out what's going on, I'll be back in touch with Josh and Clay to see if they've got new intel and where they're going." He started leaning back in his seat, but then jerked back forward, looking at him. "And, boss? Silas was right. You're the right man for the job, and we've got this."

Lydia's body lurched forward but was held in place by a seatbelt and shoulder straps. Slowly wakening, she blinked heavy-lidded eyes, wondering about the strange dream she had had. Taking in her surroundings, she scrunched her brow, confused. *Why am I in a plane? Where am I going?*

Her mouth was dry and as she tried to lift her head,

she found she could barely move it. Her gaze landed on her hands in her lap, her wrists taped together. She stared at them, not understanding what was happening. After a moment, her memories started slowly moving back into her mind. Struggling with her wrists, her arm ached, and she winced. *That's right—I was drugged. Twice! That's why my mouth is dry.*

As the plane lurched again, she looked in front of her frantically and saw a bag. Reaching out, she snagged it with difficulty, just in time to throw up.

"Shit! Thank God I took that gag off!"

As she retched into the bag, she tried to ignore the fear that was clawing at her throat. Leaning back, she had to lift both hands to wipe her mouth, then twisted to look at the man sitting beside her. She did not recognize him, other than knowing it was the man who had shown up at her house.

"Why?" she croaked.

He looked at her and the vomit-filled bag in her lap with disgust." Shifting his gaze back up to her face, he shrugged, and said, "A job. You're a means to an end."

Not having any idea what he meant, she leaned her head back, willing her stomach to settle as the plane finally lurched one more time and came to a stop. She wanted to ask where they were, but fear kept her quiet. As her still-fuzzy brain continued to slowly process what was going on, she remembered hearing the word Denver. Looking out the small window next to her, she saw a large airport to the right, but was unable to determine which one it was. Not knowing how long she had been unconscious didn't help.

She looked at the back of the pilot, but he never turned around to acknowledge her. *Does he know what's happening to me?* Glancing back down at her taped wrists, she surmised the pilot must know something was going on and either was not going to help or, was in on it, as well.

The pilot called several signals into his radio, then said to the man sitting next to her, "I've got to refuel and check the plane. There's a bathroom inside the building. You want to get her in there and give her a break before we take off again?"

"I'm in charge here, so don't give me your advice."

"And I'm the pilot, and we don't leave until I say we do. I don't want her getting sick in my plane anymore. I agreed to fly, but I'm not going to torture her. Let her go to the bathroom, let her get cleaned up, and give her something to drink. After all, you're supposed to deliver her alive. Sick or dead isn't going to get you anything."

Her eyes widened at the pilot's words, but she remained still. The man next to her grumbled, but he acquiesced. Turning toward her, he said, "There's no one around except you, me, and the pilot. I'm gonna let you out, and we're gonna walk to the bathroom. I'll undo your hands, but I'm going to be right with you. Just do what you gotta do and we'll be on our way."

Still uncertain, she nodded. He climbed out of the plane first, then turned around and assisted her down. She glanced around while walking toward the building, but he appeared to be correct. She did not see anyone else. Entering the small building, she saw an empty office and another door, but nothing else.

He opened the door first and looked in. Turning toward her, he said, "There's no window, so there's nothing you can do except go to the bathroom. If you need to drink some water, slurp it out of the sink with your hands."

He cut the tape binding her wrists, and she immediately started to rub the soreness. Putting his hand between her shoulder blades, he gave her a little push. She stepped in and closed the door, locking it swiftly. Taking in the space, a toilet and sink were the only items in the small room. Quickly using the toilet, she washed her hands and did as he suggested, slurping some water to rinse her mouth before drinking. Splashing her face with cold water helped to center her focus.

She glanced around but he had been right...there was no way out. He banged on the door, and she opened it, understanding that escape, at this point, was not likely. As they stepped out of the building, she felt a hard object at her back and his hot breath at her ear.

"You make a sound, Doc, and you're dead. Don't push me on this. Now walk straight to the plane and get back in."

She began to shiver, uncertain if it were the effects of the drugs he had given her, adrenaline, or fear. As she felt a tear slide down her cheek, she figured it was a combination of all three.

Climbing back into the plane, she begged, "Please don't bind my wrists again. I'm inside the plane and can't go anywhere. I don't want to die, so I'm not going to try to fight you or the pilot."

It was the most she had said to him the entire time she had been in his presence, and she had no idea what he would say. Silently praying that he would agree, she was shocked when he gave a short nod.

Once they were buckled in, the pilot climbed back into the cockpit, continuing to ignore her. She turned to look out her window, seeing the sun slowly sinking, casting shadows from the airport. Wondering where they were going and what was going to happen to her, her heart jumped when she heard the pilot radio to the tower that his destination was Seattle. *Seattle? What are they going to do with me in Seattle? And why?*

23

As soon the wheels touched down in Denver, Eric was already on the phone with Mace. "Please, God, tell me you've got some news.

"It looks like Robert Edger has been using the money from Korea to fund Foundation for Liberating Animals activities, both legal and otherwise. It also looks like it's been his sole source of income."

"Why was he going to take Dr. Hughley? As far as I know, his group just wants to disrupt and terrorize. Kidnapping her was not going to shut down the NBAF."

"I don't know, Eric," Mace said. "My educated guess is, somebody has been paying him to fund the FLA and is now holding that over his head in order to get him to do their dirty work. I'm going to have Josh send Chris all the information that we've been able to dig up. You can get it to DHS."

Thanking Mace profusely, he got off the phone and

turned toward Chris. "You're about to get an entire file from Josh. Forward it to Silas and Paul."

The Cessna coasted to a stop, and the pilot turned and looked back toward him. "I'm gonna refuel just in case we need to go somewhere else. As soon as you find out where we're going, let me know, so I can file the report."

Nodding, his phone rang, and Eric looked at the caller ID, seeing Logan's name listed. Picking up, he prompted, "Yeah?"

"I've been keeping track of what's going on at the Denver airport. A small, four-seater Cessna came in almost two hours ago. The time didn't look right so I checked, and it looks like the pilot filed a false report. My guess is that he's the one we're looking for. He left an hour ago, headed to Seattle, Washington."

"Seattle? What the fuck?" During the flight, he had managed to keep his emotions from boiling over, but his normally calm, focused mind was on overload. He had never been in a position where the mission concerned somebody he cared deeply about. "God-damnit," he cursed. "Seattle can only mean one thing. They want to get her out of the country."

Logan agreed, saying, "That was my assessment too. I'm so sorry, man. But I'm going to coordinate getting everybody to Seattle. I'm coming there as well."

It took a second for Logan's words to sink in, but when they did, he jolted. "What? You're coming?"

"Already got my bird ready and kissed Vivian good-bye. I'll be there about the same time that you will."

His heart squeezed and, this time, it was not

thinking about Lydia. It was the knowledge that he had men—good men—who were joining his team for no other reason than just because they wanted to help. His voice choked, but he managed to get out, "Thanks, man. I've got no words. Just thanks."

"I've got your pilot's information. I'll be in touch."

Chris had heard the conversation, so as the pilot stuck his head back into the plane, he gave him the destination. As Eric disconnected from his call with Logan, the pilot looked at him and asked, "Seattle?" Seeing his nod, he said, "I'll file the report. You best take a quick break now, 'cause we should be able to be in the air within ten minutes."

Rank was standing at the luggage claim area of the Los Angeles airport and, to the casual observer, he was nothing more than another Hollywood star or wannabe. Tall, muscular, sandy blond hair hanging to his shoulders, dressed in jeans, boots, and a T-shirt that stretched across his torso. He pushed his sunglasses up on his head and smiled widely as another man approached.

Bart was so similar in size and appearance that, when they were SEALs together, people assumed they were brothers, if not twins. Bart's hair was shorter, but to the casual observer, that was the only difference.

They clasped hands then pulled each other in for a man hug, slaps on the back ensuing.

"Good to see you again, Bart. Wish it was under

better circumstances. I sure as hell hate to have broken up your second honeymoon with Faith."

Bart nodded, replying, "Good to see you, too. Don't worry about the honeymoon. We were on our last day, and Faith was itching to get back to the kids. I just sent her on to Virginia and changed my ticket to head out here." Grinning, he added, "I understand you and Helena are now engaged?"

He nodded, smiling in return. "Couldn't get a ring on her finger fast enough."

They headed out of the terminal and to his car, but instead of leaving the airport area, he drove them to the far edge of the field and through a guarded gate. On the drive over, he filled Bart in on what he knew. "Just got word they're heading to Seattle. Eric's assumption is that they may be trying to get Lydia out of the country."

"Do you think the kidnappers know they've got the wrong person yet?"

"I don't think so. If they did, I don't think they'd keep going to Seattle. They'd probably...well, shit. You know, they'd probably kill her."

"Fuckin', hell," Bart breathed, rubbing his hand over his face.

"Logan Bishop is flying his bird in from Montana. He's going to meet us in Seattle."

"No shit? Preacher? Damn, we're getting the whole team back together again. It's the only good thing about this mess, but it makes me wonder why the hell we only get together when something happens to someone we care about. We gotta start visiting each other when it's just kicking back and talking over the old days."

He nodded. "Don't know how much our women want to hear about the old days, but you're right. We really do need to get together more often."

He parked, and they alighted from his vehicle, both grabbing their bags on the way. Walking toward another plane, they shook hands with the pilot.

"I've already filed our destination for Seattle," the pilot said. "I'll let you know that some bad weather is coming into that area. Strong winds and heavy rain. There's the possibility that we might get diverted."

Rank rubbed his chin, and asked, "Is there any chance that the plane we're chasing could get diverted as well? And how would we know?"

"I've got the call sign for the plane that it appears they're taking. If they get diverted, I'm gonna know about it."

Nodding, he said, "All right, we're ready." Looking over at Bart, he clapped him on the shoulder. "Let's go do this."

Paul got on the phone and talked to his counterpart in Seattle. "Looks like the final destination is your city. Be ready to intercept the plane when it lands. Do everything you can to keep him from knowing what you're doing so that Lydia Hughes is unharmed. There's a DHS contract team on their way as well, but I'd rather everything be handled internally, if possible. I don't care what happens to that maniac, Robert Edger, but we need to find out who he's working for, so take him alive."

Lydia was leaning against the edge of her headrest, glad that her wrists were no longer bound but still feeling nauseous and slightly groggy from the effects of the drugs she had been given her.

The face of her daughter came to mind, and she wondered how terrified Caroline would be when someone finally told her that her mother was missing. Squeezing her eyes tightly, she prayed that Caroline would find the strength to go on if this all ended badly.

Eric moved through her mind, as well. They were so new. *How many times would he call before he gives up on me because he hadn't received an answer?*

The rain outside the plane had been splattering against the window for an hour, and she felt the jerking movement as wind gusts slammed into them. She wondered about any long-lasting effects from the drugs, but if they were going to kill her, what would it matter? *If they were going to kill me, wouldn't they have already done it? Why on earth kidnap me in the first place?* Fear lapped at her again, and she shivered. Letting out a ragged breath, she crossed her arms tightly around her waist, praying for strength.

Her musings were interrupted as the man sitting next to her barked out, "What do you mean, we can't get there?"

"Do you see the fuckin' rain?" the pilot responded. "Can you feel how I have to fight to hold this plane steady? There's a goddamn storm going on outside, and we're not going to make it to Seattle!"

"You can't tell me they shut down the Seattle airport—"

"I didn't say they shut it down. I said we can't make it. This isn't a fucksing Boeing 737. This size aircraft can't fly in the same weather that a jet can. I'm looking to see where I can land. We're close to Portland, so that'll have to do."

"I'm expected in Seattle," her captor said, his voice now sounding whiny.

"Then when we land in Portland, you can just tell whoever you were supposed to meet that we didn't make it. Once the storm ends, we can leave Portland and fly to Seattle, but I'm not doing that until it's safe. Hell, the airport wouldn't let us leave anyway until the storm passes."

She remained quiet during the argument, keeping her head in the same position it had been, but slanting her eyes to the side. She watched her kidnapper as he rubbed his hands together, apparently nervous, and she assumed he was trying to figure out what to do. The swaying movement of the plane worsened her nausea, but she tried to force her thoughts to what she might accomplish once they landed in Portland.

Maybe I can run. Maybe they'll fall asleep and I can get away. Maybe we'll be close to other people, and I can alert them to what's happening.

Feeling slightly better at the possibilities, she shifted her legs, her body stiff and aching. She could feel the kidnapper's eyes on her, so she only moved enough to get more comfortable. His temper seemed rather volatile, and she did not want to engage him in conversation again, so she kept her eyes toward the window.

He mumbled, "More trouble than you're worth, Doc."

She wondered why he continued to refer to her as 'Doc', but considered that was more impersonal than using her actual name. As the pilot began the plane's descent, she stopped wondering the *whys* of anything that had happened to her and focused on not throwing up again as the winds rocked the plane.

"We're not gonna make it to Seattle," Eric's pilot called back.

His heart sunk, his fears coming to light. He had been watching the storm increase as the winds and rain beat against the small plane and was afraid that they might not make it.

"But if we can't, that means they can't either," the pilot added.

"Where are we? Where can we get to? Better yet, where do you think they are?"

"Portland. It looks like most small planes are being sent to Portland. I'm radioing my contact to see if he can locate the plane that Lydia was on. If they're stranded in Portland, we can get to them. Hell, we'll be there in about fifteen minutes."

Eric's mind quickly recalculated what needed to be done. Giving the pilot the information for Rank and

Bart's plane, as well as Logan's helicopter, he said, "I need you to let them know to divert to Portland."

He listened as the pilot followed his instructions and then began their descent. Looking over at Chris, he noted the young man's hair standing on end, his hand having run through it more than usual. Chris' face showed fatigue, and his normally wired energy was subdued. He almost chuckled, thinking that if he looked in a mirror himself, he would appear very similar.

The landing was rough considering the wind gusts, but the pilot handled the aircraft like an expert, and they were soon taxiing to a small hangar.

"I've contacted my DHS supervisor," the pilot said. "Immigration and Customs was on the alert in Seattle, and it appears that the ones here in Portland have just been notified."

Eric's chest tightened once more, and he growled, "So, with the delay, Robert could've slipped through their blockade."

Once inside the hangar, he and Chris alighted from the aircraft. His eyes immediately landed on the two large men stalking toward him, their faces tense. Throwing his hand out, he reached the first one, and said, "Bart, no words, man. Just my eternal thanks."

Bart pulled him in for a hug, then stepped back allowing the same for Rank. Turning, he introduced them to Chris, and then his eyes alighted on another man walking from the back. Muscular as well, Logan had more sinewy leanness than bulk. His dark hair was longer than he remembered, his face more lined. And yet, even in the tense situation, he saw ease in all three men. The women in their lives had to be the reason. When he got Lydia back maybe, one day, he would exude that same peace.

Moving to embrace Logan as well, they all stood in a circle, and he asked, "Did we lose them here?"

Logan, not mincing words, replied, "They had already landed by the time DHS got the word that they were probably going to come here."

"Fuck!" he and Chris cursed at the same time.

"There is good news though," Logan added. "They got a rental. It's a small car, not good for the weather in this region, but it was the only thing that was left. The rental associate remembers the man, and when presented with a photograph of Robert, she confirmed it was him."

"And Lydia?" he asked, anxious for the answer.

"Negative. Sorry, man. I know this is hard."

He watched as Chris stepped to the side and sat cross-legged on the floor of the hangar, his computer in his lap. "Which rental company?" Chris asked.

"Star Rentals," Logan replied. "They're a local company. It seems with so many people landing here in Portland because of the storm, all the other major car rental dealers were out of stock." Logan grinned, adding, "They've got GPS on all their cars."

Chris looked up, and smirked, "Excellent."

The other men regarded Chris with interest as he began typing rapidly. Eric smiled a little, remembering what he had thought of him when they first met. But he had proven himself to be a priceless asset in all this... and a good friend.

MARYANN JORDAN

After less than a minute, Chris looked up and held his gaze. "They're the most expensive car rental business in the area, which is probably why they were the only ones that had a car left. Lucky for us, though, because tracking GPS on vehicles is a piece of cake."

Eric's heart leaped for the first time that day. Logan knelt to the floor next to Chris and watched him work. Chris began tapping on his computer again, with Logan staring over his shoulder making suggestions.

"Bingo!" Chris looked up with a large smile on his tired face. "Boss, we've got 'em. Looks like he's driving to Seattle, but there must've been an accident on one of the main highways because he's taking a back road."

"What if they leave the car?" Rank asked.

Logan and Chris looked at each other and grinned, then in unison said, "Cell phone." Chris continued the explanation, saying, "He had to leave his cell number on the rental agreement. We've pinged it and, right now, they're in the same place, so he's in the car with his phone. But if they dump the car," he grinned up at Eric, "we've still got him."

He looked at his team, some old and some new, and said, "Number one objective is to get to Lydia and get her out safe. DHS wants Robert, and I do too, but never forget that's secondary to her."

He had already looked over and spied the two, large SUVs and knew that his team would have them well-equipped. As they all nodded their agreement, he called out, "Let's roll!"

"Hell, yeah," echoed inside the hangar.

Exhaustion threatened to overtake Lydia, but she was terrified of closing her eyes. The small rental car bounced along some of the rough roads as her kidnapper tried to see through the heavy rain. Night had descended, but even if it had been the bright of day, she doubted she would've been able to see much. Rain pelted the car so furiously that with the wipers going at full blast, visibility was almost nil.

At first, she was grateful to not be on another airplane, but now she despised the jolting potholes that he seemed to be able to find with ease. Her geography was not strong, but she knew they had landed in Portland and were now trying to drive north to Seattle. She assumed they were surrounded by forests, but it was hard to tell in the powerful rainfall.

She had glanced at the dashboard when they first got in, observing that this car had GPS as part of its package, but he did not seem to know that. He drove with his left hand on the steering wheel and his right hand holding his phone, alternating between cursing at the screen and looking out the window.

Uncertainty filled her, not knowing what to do. Given the weather conditions, it was dangerous for him to keep looking at his phone, driving one handed. Already, more than once, they had almost careened off the road. But if she tried to help him with the GPS, would that simply get her to her unknown destination quicker? Not having any idea why she was being

kidnapped or where she was being taken, she had little
cause to make things easier for him.

She shivered slightly, having become soaked while
getting from the plane to the rental car. Glancing to the
side, she knew he shared her predicament. He finally
shivered as well, and she was grateful when he turned
the knob to allow heat to move through the automobile.

The backend fishtailed as he took a turn too quickly,
and she grabbed hold of the door handle for support,
her heart racing.

"Get your hand away from there," he growled.
"Trying to jump out of this car now would be stupid.
And as a doctor, I can't imagine you're stupid."

"I'm not trying to jump out. I'm just trying to hang
on." She had said very little during her ordeal, and her
voice sounded unfamiliar to her—raspy and hoarse. She
cleared her throat and considered speaking more, but
another fishtail kept her quiet.

He over-corrected, and the car began to lurch sideways, the wheels unable to grab the surface. She
screamed as they spun around in a circle, before sliding
off into a ditch by the side of the road. The rear of the
car went into the ditch first, causing the entire vehicle
to tilt upward. They bounced and rumbled downward
until finally jolting to a stop with a loud crunch. Unable
to see outside, she had no idea if they were near a creek
or, God forbid, a river.

The man beside her began cursing unmercifully, his
fists pounding the steering wheel.

She continued to shiver but, this time, it was not
from the cold, but the fear. Still too afraid to ask him

any questions, she remained quiet, thankful when no water began to seep into the vehicle. The sounds of their fast breathing filled the air, and she swung her head to the side to see what he was going to do.

She startled when he began speaking, not having noticed he had dialed someone on his phone.

"I was on Highway Five, but there was an accident this side of Olympia, and I had to get off. I remember seeing a sign for Lambert's Corner but then turned off on another road. I think we're near some national forest. I was using my phone to get me to Seattle, but I can't see shit, and these roads are terrible. We've gone into a ditch."

He must have had the sound turned up on his phone because she could hear the other person clearly.

"I have been waiting at the rendezvous point for two hours. I do not like to be kept waiting."

"Did you hear me? I said we've gone off the road. We're in a fuckin' ditch!"

"How is the doctor? Is she all right?"

The inside of the car was so dark, but she could see his face illuminated by the screen on his phone. He turned toward her, his eyes raking over her. "Yeah, she's fine. It's not like the car crumpled or anything. We're just stuck in a fucking ravine."

"You imbecile—"

"Don't take that tone with me. I've been up and down on goddamn flights, doing everything you told me to do. If we get caught, I'm the one that will hang because I'm the one that took her."

"You're being paid very well to do exactly what I tell

you to do."

"That money won't do me any good if I end up in prison for kidnapping. I'll let you know right now, if I go down, you go down."

Laughter was heard coming over the phone line, and the other man said, "I'm outside your laws. I'll be long gone if anything happens. But enough about this, we'll come up with a new rendezvous point. Where are you now?"

Mumbling, "Fuck if I know," he jabbed at his phone's GPS several more times, and then replied, "Okay, I got it. We're north of Black Lake, about two miles south of Highway 101."

A heavy sigh was heard, and she tried to still her heavy breathing so that she could continue to listen.

"I've located a small hotel with cabins not too far from you. You will take her and walk there. It will probably take me close to two hours to drive there." Chuckling again, the man said, "With you going on foot, I'll probably get there before you."

Arguing, her kidnapper groused, "How do you expect me to walk in the dark, in the rain, dragging the doc along with me?"

She listened as the voice from the phone dropped an octave. "That is not my problem. You are to be there and make sure she's with you. I want her alive and well."

Her breath left her in a whoosh as she heard that she was not going to be killed, but she still could not understand why anyone wanted her. Before she had a chance to process that further, her arm was grabbed in a tight hold, and she jumped.

"You heard that. We've got no fuckin' choice but to get out in this."

He squeezed harder, and she whimpered, "Please, you're hurting me."

"I'll do a lot more than that if you give me any problems," he warned, but loosened his hold slightly.

"So, we're going to walk? In this storm?" she asked, her voice trembling as her head nodded slightly toward the rain pouring on the outside.

"We've got no choice."

She heard the resignation in his voice as he sighed heavily. He let go of her wrist and twisted around to the back seat, grabbing a bag. Digging into it, he pulled out duct tape.

"No, oh please God, no. Don't tape me up again," she begged.

"I can't take the risk of you running away from me."

Bravery born out of desperation, she said, "Where am I going to go? We're in the middle of nowhere, in the pouring rain, in the dark. There are woods all around and God knows what kind of wild animals."

She observed his jaw tightening and held her breath, terrified that he would grab her and tape her wrists together again. Finally, after what seemed like an eternity, he dropped the tape back into the bag.

"Don't make me regret this," he threatened. "Now, let's get going."

Nodding with gratitude over being able to use her arms and hands, she opened her door and tumbled outside. She immediately slipped on the wet leaves, going down hard on her hands and knees. The rain was pelting down so fiercely, she was drenched within a moment. She heard him coming around the front of the vehicle and scrambled to her feet. Pushing her wet hair away from her eyes, she began the climb up the incline toward the road.

Unable to see, she felt her way through the leaves over the rough rocks, feeling his presence right behind her. Finally touching asphalt, she hauled herself up the final few feet to get to the pavement. Still kneeling on all fours, now on the road, she was not sure her legs would hold her upright, but the kidnapper gave her no choice. He grabbed her roughly by the arm again, this time jerking her upward. She weaved back and forth for a few seconds before gathering the strength in her legs to stand on her own.

"I've got it."

He let go of her arm, mumbling to himself. She looked back and forth in either direction, not remembering ever having been in such blackness before. If it was not for the occasional flash of lightning, she would have no idea of her surroundings.

Her kidnapper looked equally confused, examining first the road and then the pitch-black ravine. "We went over this side, so we must've been going in that direction." He lifted his hand toward the left, and ordered, "Move."

Stumbling alongside him, having no clue where she was going, she could only pray they would keep her alive long enough for someone to find her. But with each step, she wondered how that could possibly happen.

25

The two upgraded Land Rovers sped down the highway, Rank at the wheel of one, with Bart riding shotgun, and Logan driving the other, with Eric and Chris. The tires handled the wet pavement with no problem, and the Xenon headlights cut through the darkness with ease. The storm had not ceased, but Eric had complete confidence that Rank and Logan would be able to handle the vehicles.

With that thought in mind, he looked over at Logan and said, "I have no idea how you were able to get these vehicles on such short notice, but you always were a logistics genius."

A man of few words, Logan's lips curved slightly at the praise, and he gave a quick nod.

From the backseat, Chris called out, "Boss, it's just as we thought might happen. Robert's vehicle signal is no longer with his cell phone signal. The vehicle signal is just up ahead."

"And the cell?" he asked, as he twisted around to look into the backseat at Chris.

"About two miles up the road."

Logan communicated with Rank and both SUVs slowed. Even in the storm, it was not difficult for this trained group of soldiers to see that a vehicle had gone over the side of the road.

"Fuck," he yelled, as he threw open his door.

Rank drove his vehicle to the edge, his headlights beaming through the heavy rain, illuminating the area but not down the ravine. Bart and Logan followed Eric over the side, both with their military-grade flashlights revealing the car at the bottom.

Rushing to the car, Eric shined his light inside, but found it empty. As Bart came up behind him, he said, "There's no blood on the inside. They must've slid off and started walking on foot."

"Where the hell are they going?" Bart asked.

Logan jerked his hat off and swiped at the water streaming down his face, before replacing his hat on his head. "We're only about two miles away from the next intersection, where there's a larger road that meets up with this one. If they were heading in that direction, they might be hoping to get to a phone or to shelter."

Chris called out, "There's a small hotel there, with cabins for rooms."

"That would be perfect," Bart said. "Less chance of someone noticing them."

He stood silently for a few seconds, gathering his thoughts. "This makes me wonder if they still don't realize they have the wrong person. If the kidnapper knew that, I would think he would have just left Lydia here, if he would've even brought her this far. As long as he doesn't know that, that gives us more time to get to her and for her to be safe."

"I agree," Logan said. "If they're on foot in this weather, they're not going very fast."

Bart looked at his watch, and said, "If we're estimating the time based on when they got to Portland, we should be coming upon them very soon."

"We need to rely on Chris to keep track of where we are and the cell phone signal," Eric said. "We want to get close, but we don't want them to see our headlights or hear us. If Robert gets desperate enough, who knows what he'll do."

The three agreed and began the ascent back up to the road. Quickly reporting to the others, Chris immediately began tapping in the coordinates on his computer.

Looking up, Chris grinned, and said, "Got 'em. Looks like they're very close to the intersection. When we get closer, I'll be able to see where they are."

Eric shook his head and tried to keep his heartbeat steady as he said, "Robert would never let her get near anyone. My guess is that he's gonna leave her outside while he checks in." He looked around at the others. "Ready?"

Once more, 'Hell, yeahs' rang out in the storm.

Lydia could not remember ever being so cold. Her

clothes were soaked, the scrubs clinging to her skin and making it difficult to walk. Even though her scrubs were of a thick, cotton material, they provided no protection or warmth in the storm. She had thought earlier, on one of the many plane trips, that she was glad she had worn a long sleeve T-shirt underneath her short-sleeved scrub but, at this point in her nightmare, it was only one more article of clothing to be soaked in cold rain.

Occasionally, she would lift a hand to swipe at the rain pounding her face. The first couple of times she did it, she spied her kidnapper watching her carefully. *He probably thinks I'm ready to attack him.* She choked back a snort, wishing she could attack him. But, right now, she was incapable of defending herself in any way.

As they continued trudging down the road, she observed his footsteps were becoming less sure. He began to stagger more than walk. The black that surrounded them, which had been so frightening earlier, began to feel strangely comforting. Almost like the night was blanketing her. *I must be losing my mind...or dying of hypothermia. Slowly.* No other thought could enter her mind, other than moving one foot in front of the other.

She staggered, falling to her hands and knees on the pavement. Exhausted, frozen, and emotionally spent, she pleaded, "I can't. I can't do this." All she wanted to do was curl up and not move, preferably in front of a warm fire, but she would take the wet pavement if that was all she had.

"It's there. It's fuckin' over there," he said through chattering teeth.

Too tired to lift her head, she winced as he grabbed her arm and jerked her upward. Blinking as the rain continued to hit her face, she saw the faint glow of a light up ahead.

"Let's go. We're getting closer."

She heard the renewed fervor in his voice and assumed he was buoyed by the almost completed journey. She wondered if the man they were going to meet was already there and, if so, what would become of her.

They approached the light but before getting too close, he pulled her over to the side of the road. "We're going to swing around toward the back. I gotta go check things out. I gotta make sure it's the right place."

He clamped his hand around her arm and began to drag her through the woods, circling closer toward the building. Staggering even more, she tripped over roots and pushed through small branches. The rain was less punishing underneath the trees, but the terrain was more treacherous than the road.

Looking to the side, she could see the small building, the lights from inside pouring through the windows. A neon light flickered to the side of the door, advertising Black Lake Cabin Hotel. *Light. Dry. Warm.* As much as she hated going with him, her feet continued forward, wanting to get to that place where she could find comfort.

As they rounded the back, he pulled her to a stop, and she watched in horror as he pulled the tape from his pocket. "No," she cried, her chest heaving, her struggles going unheeded as he easily jerked her toward a tree.

"I can't take you with me. I can't risk it." He jerked her closer to the tree, pulling her hands on either side of the trunk so that she hugged it. She tried to dig her feet in, to pull away, but the wet, slippery leaves underneath did not allow her much resistance. He held her hands on either side of the small trunk, clutching them in one of his much larger ones as he pulled on the tape with his teeth, loosening the end. With some difficulty, he managed to wrap it around her wrists a couple of times.

When he let go, she struggled roughly, but to no avail, tears streaming down her face. He reached into his pocket and pulled out a handkerchief, and she sagged, defeated. His hands shook as he tied the gag into her mouth, and it brought her a small measure of comfort, to know that he was as cold and miserable as she was.

Without another word, he walked away and disappeared around the side of the building. Leaning her face against the rough bark of the tree, the canopy doing little to shield her from the rain, unable to stop herself, she cried.

She had no idea how much time had passed when she felt the tape roughly ripped off her wrists. Stumbling back, she caught herself before she fell completely, wrapping her arms tightly around her middle.

"Come on," he ordered, his hand around her arm once more.

He half-dragged and half-carried her down a lighted path to the farthest cabin. After knocking three times, he entered and pulled her forward. A blast of warm heat hit her, and her legs gave out from under her. She slumped to the floor, relishing the feel of a warm, dry room.

He bent, and untied the handkerchief from around her mouth, before threatening, "I'm only doing this because we're not close to any other cabin. But you make a peep, and I'll hogtie you up."

Too exhausted to consider any other recourse, she simply nodded, grateful to not be bound. She pushed her dripping hair from her face and tried to focus on the room, looking for the source of the heat. There was a register in the ceiling near the chair by the bed, and she thought about trying to crawl over to sit under it. Looking in the other direction, she spied the door to the bathroom and that called to her more urgently.

"Can I...use...the...bathroom?" she asked, her chattering teeth making it difficult to speak. "Pl...please."

He stared for a moment, then checked it out and came back, relenting. "The window is painted shut, so don't get any funny ideas."

She nodded and stood on shaky legs, grabbing the door frame as she entered and then shutting the door. It was hard to peel her sopping pants down her legs, and even harder to get them back on, but she managed. Finishing her business, she ran the water in the sink until it was warm and held her hands under the stream. Finding a washcloth, she wet it and luxuriated in the feel of the warmth on her face.

Hearing voices from inside the room, she froze, panicked. *Who else is here? Someone from the hotel?*

Please, God. Opening the door a crack and peeking through, her hopes were dashed as her gaze landed on a man dressed in an expensive black raincoat and fedora.

She gasped, recognizing him instantly. "Ji-Ho?"

"You?" he asked, his eyes boring into her, appearing equally stunned.

Stepping out slowly, she watched in fascination as his expression morphed from shocked to enraged. He swung his head slowly from her to her kidnapper.

"Robert," he spoke with surprising calm. "Can you explain why you have *her* here?"

Robert. It dawned on her that she had never asked his name, mostly out of fear. She shifted her attention to him, seeing his brow knit in confusion.

"Her? What the hell are you talking about? You wanted Dr. Linda Hughley, so I brought you Dr. Linda Hughley!"

"That's not Linda Hughley," Ji-Ho bit out, his face red as his arm swung out to indicate her. 'That's Dr. *Lydia Hughes.*"

Robert's gaze shifted to her, and dawning slid over her at the same time it obviously did him. *He didn't want me...he took the wrong person!* Thoughts raced through her mind like cars on a racetrack, all moving quickly and passing each other.

I'm not who they wanted. Why did they want Linda? Why is Ji-Ho involved? What will they do with me now?

It was the last thought that caused her blood to freeze in her veins, knowing they would never let her live to tell what had happened. Her lungs felt incapable of drawing in enough air, but she could not take her eyes from the scene playing out in front of her.

"You have been nothing but a problem since I met you."

"No, Hyun-Gi...no, she's the right one," Robert sputtered, staring at her. "She never said..."

"I don't understand," she whispered, uncertain of her voice. "Why..." Her gaze dropped to the floor, and she pressed her fingers to her lips in horror as the reality of the situation hit.

"This waste of a man is the head of the Foundation for Liberating Animals."

Looking up at Robert, she assessed him with new eyes. She recognized the organization and the terrorist tactics they used. He was the one behind it all? She didn't trust herself to speak, but she did not have to worry about that, because Ji-Ho continued.

"He was paid well to serve us and, as you can now surmise, he was supposed to take the head of the NBAF, not a low-level veterinarian."

"I don't...I don't understand. Why do you need Linda?" She shook her head slowly, "I don't..."

He held her gaze, before replying. "Dr. Hughley has specific knowledge...knowledge my country wants."

Her brow scrunched, her head shaking back and forth repeatedly. "South Korea?"

"No," he bit out, his tone indicating his frustration. "I'm North Korean. My name is not Ji-Ho, it is Hyun-Gi, as Robert has mentioned. I'm a scientist from North Korea...not a journalist. We need the research she has perfected, and my country paid well for us to have access to it. She gave very little away during the seminar, so I was given instructions to just take her."

"Take her where? None of this makes sense," she cried, no longer caring if her questions made her captors angry.

"Back," he said. "Back with me. If she did not cooperate, well, my organization can be very persuasive."

At this, her mouth hung open, the impact of his words hitting her.

"This is pointless," Robert said, drawing an immediate glare from Hyun-Gi. "We need to figure out what to do with her."

"You've made a mess of things, and now I have to clean it up," Hyun-Gi said, his voice soft, but just as frightening.

Without pre-amble, he pulled out a small gun from his pocket and lifted it, shooting Robert point-blank in the chest.

She screamed, jumping back as Robert fell to the floor with a thud, a look of surprise etched on his face as blood ran from his body.

Her body shook, more than when she was cold, and she stared up at Hyun-Gi and began to shake her head back and forth. "No, please no." His jaw ticked, and it seemed an eternity before he lowered his weapon but kept it in his hand.

"I can still use you," he said, bending over to pick up his coat. "You're my ticket out of here."

Waving his gun, he ordered, "Move. My car is out front."

Her legs barely holding her up, she avoided looking

at Robert's body on the floor as she made her way to the door. She stumbled but righted herself at the sight of the gun near her. "Where are we going?"

His lips curved but he did not answer. Jerking his head to the side, he indicated for her to go back outside. Opening the door, she was immediately hit with the rain blowing in. Shivering as they ran to his car, she wondered when her nightmare would end…and what would be at the end.

26

"Turn here!" Chris yelled from the back seat. Logan jerked the steering wheel, and the back end of the SUV skidded slightly on the wet pavement, its all-terrain tires quickly digging in and shooting them forward.

Eric leaned forward, staring out the windshield as the wipers slung the rain to the side, giving him an instant to see clearly before visual was once again compromised. A small building with lights and neon signs declaring it a cabin rental was on the left, but Chris directed them down the small lane to the right. Out of his peripheral vision, he saw headlights pulling away from one of the cabins nearby and moving toward the street, but their destination was the furthest cabin.

Cutting the headlights, Logan crept forward, and Rank maneuvered his SUV close by. Alighting from the vehicles silently, they circled around the final cabin. The windows were covered with curtains, but light was shining from inside. His mind was fully on the success of the mission, anxious to see Lydia but wanting to make sure she was rescued unharmed.

Chris stayed in the vehicle while everyone else encircled the cabin. There was no back door, but they made sure all windows were covered. Weapons drawn, Rank moved to the front door, prepared to kick the door in if necessary, but reached and tried the doorknob first. Eyebrows lifted, he shot a look toward him and received a nod.

Throwing open the door, his weapons drawn, Rank moved in, and Eric immediately followed. A man's body was flat on its back on the floor, surrounded by blood.

Rushing over, he looked down and recognized Robert, dead from a gunshot wound to the chest. Eyes quickly scanning the space, he saw water puddles on the floor but no evidence of Lydia. As Logan and Bart came around from the back sides, Rank moved out of the bathroom, shaking his head.

"No sign of her."

"Fuck," he cursed. "Of course, his fuckin' cell phone is here with him and we've got no idea where Lydia is!"

Chris came across the radio, and said, "According to my satellite pictures there was only the one car in this area and that's the one that left just as we were coming in."

They all looked at each other for a split second before darting back out into the rain toward the SUVs. Eric ordered, "Logan, call this into Silas so he can notify the local police. But let him know we're after Lydia. Whoever shot Robert has taken her."

Bart and Rank climbed into their vehicle, and he,

Chris, and Logan jumped into theirs. Twisting around in the seat, he pinned Chris with a hard stare, "Pressure's on you, man. Keep track of where they're going and get us there!"

"You got it, boss. Head back out, going north," Chris said, his face a study of concentration as he stared at his computer screen. "They're only about three miles ahead and not driving very fast."

Glancing to the side, Eric opened his mouth, but Logan got there first. "No worries, we know how to drive in the dark and in the rain. We'll catch them."

"Whoever Robert was meeting knew what Linda looked like. When he recognized Robert's mistake, he shot him and took Lydia," he surmised, doing everything in his power to stay focused and not think of the new danger this put Lydia in.

"Who do you think has her?" Bart asked. "We know North Korea was aware of the abduction, but it could be anyone."

"The only person we have connected to Robert at this point is a man named Hyun-Gi. It could be him, but we don't know for sure. All we can do now is follow their trail."

From the backseat, Chris asked, "Why take her at all? If she's not who they needed, what's the purpose?"

Shaking his head slightly, his thoughts were interrupted as Chris threw out, "Take a left right here," and Logan easily maneuvered the vehicle onto the new road.

"They must be keeping her hostage because she represents safety. Whatever this person's original plan was for Linda Hughley, they've now got to keep Lydia with them as collateral to help them get away." The road became rougher, and Eric questioned out loud, "Where the fuck does this road lead?"

"If they're going by the GPS, this road is a shortcut to getting back to the highway, but it's not a good road. It's in somewhat of disrepair, and it has a one-lane bridge that goes over a body of water. They call it a lake, but it's real small."

"Stay sharp," he said to those in his own vehicle and, with the radio, to Rank and Bart in the other. "Desperate people make mistakes, and this person has got to be desperate."

He knew his words were true, but the fear that was snaking through his body was that Lydia would be caught in the crosshairs of that desperation.

Lydia watched as Ji-Ho...Hyun-Gi...drove cautiously down the road. She had felt that Robert took unnecessary risks as he sped through the dark night in the pouring rain and wind, but then it was not an automobile accident that killed him. Instead, he died at the hands of the man sitting beside her. That thought should be sending shockwaves of fear through her and, yet, she felt strangely calm. Whether it was the shock, fatigue, or that she had somehow been transported into the set of a movie instead of reality, she did not know.

Casting her gaze to the side, she watched as Ji-Ho—Hyun-Gi, she reminded herself, gripped the steering wheel with tight concentration and wondered if he had any idea where he was going.

"Where are you taking me?" she asked.

He did not answer for a moment, focusing on the road as he made a right turn where the GPS indicated. "Someone will meet me. It was my way to get back home."

His words did not make sense, and she glanced out the windshield, thinking of where someone might possibily be waiting out here. Water was the only means of escape that she could think of. *Of course, a boat couldn't get to North Korea, so the boat would probably have to meet up with a ship somewhere.* Thinking of how Linda would have been forced to make that trip, she shuddered.

She did not know how much longer they had before they met up with his transportation, but knew she was close to the end of her line. Once there and safe, he would have no more use for her.

Grateful he had not bound her hands, her mind raced to think of escape.

"Soon," he said. "We are close."

Her attention was forced back to the road as he slowed considerably and pulled onto a small, one lane bridge. The rain had decreased slightly and with the assistance of the headlights, she was able to see they were crossing a body of water. Unable to determine if it was a lake, a river, or a bay leading to the ocean, she was flooded with the realization that this might be her only possible chance of escape.

A flash of light caught her eye through her side view

mirror, and she blinked to enhance the focus of her tired eyes. It appeared to be headlights, but the light disappeared before she could be sure. *If it was headlights in the distance behind her, then someone could see us and help.*

Hyun-Gi was not paying any attention to her, leaning forward over the steering wheel, staring out into the dark. Determined to make a move, without thinking it through any further, she quietly unbuckled her seatbelt and slammed her body toward the left, hitting him. Having the element of surprise on her side, she grabbed the steering wheel and struggled for control.

She had the advantage for only a few seconds, before he threw his hands out to fight back. With his foot on the accelerator, he sped up just as she threw her weight onto him again and jerked the steering wheel once more to the right. The sedan slammed into the guardrail, and she felt it give way as the car dangled off the bridge.

Hyun-Gi cried out, his hand meeting her face as he flailed his arms in an attempt to push her away and grab the steering wheel. As the vehicle listed to the side, he continued to turn the steering wheel, as though that would have any effect on a car whose front half was hanging off a bridge.

Filled with adrenaline and rage, she pushed herself toward the right, managing to get her hand onto the doorknob and threw open her door just as the car rocked further. They were balancing on the edge, but she flung her body out the door, desperate for escape.

She did not have far to fall, slamming into the icy cold water. The shock reverberated throughout her body, but she instinctively kicked her legs and pushed her arms so that she moved upward. Her head popped up through the surface, but the water was as inky black as the night, with only the headlights dangling from above illuminating her surroundings.

A loud crack split the air, but she was uncertain if it was a gunshot, the automobile above, or the bridge. Unwilling to wait and see, she began to move away from the bridge, hoping she was going closer to land.

She knew she had a very short time before hypothermia took over her body. With every passing second, her movements became more and more sluggish, as though she were in slow motion. Her mind began to slow down, matching her movements.

Strange, she thought, treading water instead of pushing on. *I no longer feel cold.*

27

Eric's control slipped as he spied the car on the bridge, careening from side to side before it tilted over the edge. The headlights from his vehicle illuminated the scene in front of him, and he could see the occupants inside the car fighting.

"I can't tell if it's her!" Logan called out, stopping on the bridge about twenty feet behind the car.

"It's her," he said, certainty moving through him as swiftly as fear. He leaped from the vehicle and ran forward, but he was too late. The passenger door opened, and a figure tumbled out into the black waters below.

Rank angled his vehicle so that his headlights were illuminating the water, closest to the bridge and bank. Logan rounded the driver's side, his weapon aimed sure and true, and called out to the man inside, "Hands where I can see them!"

Eric watched Ji-Ho lift his hands and immediately raced to the guardrail. There was no time to waste, so without hesitation, he dove off the side of the bridge.

He ignored the jolt of cold when his body hit the water. It may have been several years since he was a SEAL, but the training was so ingrained, it was like the time had never passed. His only priority was getting to Lydia, knowing that she was much weaker and would not be able to survive the cold.

His head broke the surface, the water illuminated by the headlights of Rank's SUV. He saw movement to his left and dove under, his strokes powerful despite the temperatures, quickly sending him in that direction.

His hands struck something soft, and he immediately grasped the material. With his free hand, he pushed up through the water, his head breaking the surface once more. Feeling Lydia limp in his arm, he easily lifted her head above the water as well.

"Lydia," he cried out, squeezing her with his arm banded about her chest.

Her body shook violently as she sputtered, sucking in a gasp of air before she began to cough. He powered toward the bank, observing Rank striding into the water to aid him. Together, they hauled her easily to shore, where Bart met them and pulled her from their arms.

He scrambled up and dropped to his knees beside her, grateful to see Chris already wrapping her in blankets. The rain had thankfully ended, but the night air was chilly, and the wind was still blowing.

He bent and picked her blanketed body up and stalked over to the SUV, where the heater was runnning. Placing her in the backseat, he climbed up next to her, and Rank jumped in the driver seat, cranking the heat up to high.

Chris jumped into the passenger seat, and said, "Bart and Logan are with her kidnapper. We've identified him as Ji-Ho. You were right, boss...he's not who he purported to be. I've called ahead to the hospital in Olympia, and they're expecting us. It should only take us twenty minutes to get there. I figured you guys can drive faster than waiting on an ambulance."

He barely heard Chris's voice, his attention focused solely on Lydia. Reaching over the back seat, he unzipped one of the duffle bags and grabbed a towel and a thick, woolen knit cap. Turning back to her, he rubbed her head briskly, before pulling the cap over her hair.

Her lips were blue, and her eyes shut. "Fuck. Chris, help."

Chris leaned between the front seats and helped hold her body, while he unwrapped her top half from the blanket and, with scissors grabbed from the medical kit, cut her scrubs away from her. Chris jerked the wet material, slinging it to the floorboard, while Eric shoved her arms into a thick, dry sweatshirt. Grabbing a dry blanket, he wrapped that around her top half.

"You going to try to get the bottom half as well?" Chris asked. "Our ETA should be fifteen minutes."

"Yeah, I want to get as much wet clothing off her as I

can." Shifting in the seat, he laid her down and breathed a sigh of relief as her eyes fluttered open. Immediately, her teeth began to chatter. "Lydia, baby can you hear me? It's Eric. I've got you and you're safe."

Her eyes jerked about wildly in the dark interior of the vehicle, and her arms began to flail. As an overhead light came on, she stilled and blinked rapidly.

Nodding his thanks toward Chris, who was holding a strong flashlight, he said, "Lydia. Look at me. Baby focus on me."

"C...c...c...cold," she stuttered, her body bucking violently with another shiver.

With Chris holding the light, Eric tugged off her shoes and socks and cut her scrub pants away as well. Her legs felt like ice as he pulled a pair of thick, cotton, sweatpants up them. Leaning over the back seat again, he found woolen socks. Keeping a running monologue going, hoping to maintain her focus, he said, "Okay, Lydia. You've got sweatpants on, and now we've got your feet covered in warm socks. Gonna get you all dry and warm, baby. You're safe, now. You're safe with me."

He encircled her in another warm blanket and assisted her to sit as he pulled her onto his lap, wrapping his arms around her. Glancing outside, he saw that they were entering civilization, and knew the hospital would be prepared for them.

"Eh...Eh...Eric?"

Her voice was weak, but her eyes were strongly focused on his face. He brought his lips directly to hers, infusing her icy skin with his warm mouth. He kissed her lightly, knowing it was still hard for her to breathe. "I'm here, baby. Hang with me, and we'll get you to the hospital."

"But…" Her voice faded as she tried to speak. Barely whispering, she managed to ask, "How?"

"Don't worry about that now, Lydia. I promise, you're safe, and I'll explain everything later." He watched as her eyes closed once again, her body wracked with shivers. Looking toward the front, he said, "Chris. Come here."

Chris scrambled his tall body between the two front seats, almost kicking Rank in the head. His eyes held questions, but instead of answering Eric motioned for him to get on the other side of Lydia. They sandwiched her body between theirs, each holding on to her cold, but now dry, body, infusing as much warmth into her as they possibly could.

Rank screeched to a halt a few minutes later in front of the ER, the inside of the SUV like an oven with the heat blasting. As the hospital personnel pulled Lydia from his arms and placed her on a stretcher, he could only pray that it had been enough.

Lydia had been conscious when she entered the hospital, but as her body warmed, she found herself drifting in and out of sleep. An older nurse named Pearl, with a sweet face and a kind manner, explained what they were doing each time she awoke.

Finally, the cold that seemed to fill her veins, freezing her from the inside out, was no longer present.

"How do you feel, Lydia?" Pearl asked.

"I'm not shivering anymore, so I figure that's a good thing."

Pearl laughed. "You're right, that's a good thing. The doctor will be in in a little bit to go over everything with you, but I can say we were able to treat the hypothermia with warm intravenous fluids, heated blankets, and the humidified oxygen that you are breathing in. Your body temperature is back to normal, and it appears that there's no skin damage or internal organ damage."

"Is it bad that I just want to stay underneath these heated blankets?" she joked, her voice still weak. "Right now, I feel like I could sleep like a hibernating bear."

Pearl laughed again and, after checking the IV, patted her blanket-buried leg, and said, "I'm gonna let your man come back now. He's been in and out checking on you with some of those other handsome men he's with. It's my understanding he's the one that rescued you when you went underwater. Mmm mmm, you're a lucky woman."

Pearl winked and walked out before Lydia could think of anything to say.

The curtain-covered doorway swished back, and Eric walked through. He immediately walked to the side of her bed and bent to place a gentle kiss on her lips.

"Thank God," he muttered, his lips still next to hers. "The last time I kissed you, your mouth was freezing, and your lips were blue."

As he leaned back, she whispered, "Eric, I don't understand any of this." Wincing as she swallowed, her throat sore, she continued, "You. I don't understand you."

He leaned back over and placed his hand on top of the blankets. "I'm reaching for your hand, but I have no idea what I'm actually touching," he grinned.

"I'm kind of mummified, aren't I?" she laughed, then glanced down. "You're near my hand. Here, let me wiggle my fingers if I can."

He must have felt the movement, because he gave her hand a squeeze over all the blankets. The smile slowly left her face, as she stared back up into his. "I feel like I've awakened from a very long dream. Some of it more like a nightmare...parts of it very foggy...some of it really nice, at least, the part about you. The problem is, Eric, I don't have a clue what's real and what's not right now."

"I promise I'll tell you everything, Lydia," he said, one hand still holding hers over the blanket and his other hand cupping her cheek, his thumb rubbing over her now-warm skin. "Just know, everything that was between us is real."

Her voice a whisper, she asked, "You're not a journalist, are you?" Seeing the hesitation on his face, she begged, "Please, tell me."

Shaking his head, he said, "No, baby, I'm not a journalist. I was on an assignment to see if I could find who was trying to breach the NBAF's security. You were never part of that mission. You were a gift I could not believe I'd been given."

She considered his words but found fatigue muddling everything in her head. Closing her eyes once more, she succumbed to sleep. Still, she heard him whisper, "Sleep for now, babe. I'll be here when you wake up."

"I can walk, you know," Lydia grumbled, but Pearl appeared to ignore her, continuing to roll her in a wheelchair out of the hospital toward a large SUV.

Eric walked along beside her and, reaching the SUV, assisted her into the backseat. The driver twisted around, and she spied a handsome man, his hair brushing his shoulders and a movie star smile beaming toward her.

"Good to see you, Lydia. I'm John Rankin. Rank, to all my friends."

Eric had already explained that some of his friends had been with him and had helped to rescue her. She smiled warmly. "It's so nice to meet you. I can't thank you enough for everything you did for me."

Rank beamed. "It was my pleasure. I would've done anything for my former SEAL commander anyway, but the chance to help him rescue you was icing on the cake."

He winked toward Eric, then turned around and began to drive. She looked over at Eric sitting next to her and lifted her eyebrow questioningly.

"We're heading to the airport, sweetheart. Rank agreed to drive us, and we'll meet up with the others there."

She was quiet for most of the drive, her mind still turbulent as she turned over the events in her head. Before she knew it, they had reached the airport, but Rank did not stop at the front. Instead, he drove around through a side gate and over to a separate hanger.

She saw a small group of men standing inside and wondered if they were Eric's friends. She did not have to wait long for the answer, as he alighted from the SUV and turned back to her, his hand extended. As he assisted her down and tucked her into his side, the other men walked over.

Rank joined them, and she blinked at the wall of masculinity presented to her. One man, very alike in looks to Rank, was introduced as Bart. A dark-haired, rather quiet man, but just as gorgeous, took her hand in his, as Eric introduced Logan.

A tall, red-haired man, grinning widely, grabbed her hand and pumped it up and down. "I'm Chris, and it's sure good to see you up and about. I was trying to follow you based on Robert's cell phone and, I gotta tell you, when we got into that bastard's room and saw him—"

"Chris," Eric growled, his voice carrying a warning.

She watched in fascination as Chris' face grew red,

from his neck all the way up to his hairline. "Oh... sorry...uh...well, I'm glad you're okay."

She could not help but laugh, and say, "There's a lot I don't remember, and some I remember that I'd like to forget. But you're right...he was a bastard."

Chris appeared pleased at her assessment and nodded once more before stepping back.

Eric gave her a squeeze, then dropped his arm from her shoulders as he stepped over to Rank. Clasping his hand, he pulled him in for a hug, saying, "I can't thank you enough."

The idea of not eavesdropping passed through her mind, but curiosity won out as she listened to Rank's reply.

"Anytime, anywhere. I still haven't forgotten how you helped with my Helena. Don't be a stranger...after all, Maine's not that far away from you."

With a smile, Eric clapped him on the shoulder before moving to Bart. "I still gotta make it down to Virginia to visit you and your family."

As Bart hugged him in return, he said, "Just like Rank said, if you need me, anytime anywhere, you know how to get hold of me."

In awe of the camaraderie she was witnessing, she was curious about Logan, but was surprised when Eric moved to him, and said, "Make sure you thank Vivian for me. Not only for letting you come to help me, but for giving me the information earlier on this case. You two make a good team."

Overcome with emotion from having been rescued by these men who had obviously put their lives on hold, she moved to each of them, offering hugs. Carefully stepping back after being enveloped by them, she leaned her weight into Eric, and he wrapped his arms around her once again.

Logan waved his goodbye, and she watched as he walked out of the hangar and climbed into his helicopter. After he had taken flight, Rank and Bart offered their farewells too, climbing into the back of another private plane.

Twisting her head around to look up at Eric, he explained, "They're both heading back to the East coast and decided to fly most of the way together."

"You all are obviously very close," she said.

He smiled at her, lifting his hand to tuck a strand of hair behind her ear. "Is that your way of asking me how I know them?"

Her lips curved, and she replied, "Okay, how about I be more direct. How do you know them?"

He sighed, and said, "I was once a Lieutenant Commander of a SEAL team. At one time, those three men served under me. I can't say that we've stayed close, but we have stayed in contact. Two of them work for security firms and another one does contracting on his own. It just so happened that they were available when I needed help."

Her brow furrowed as she pondered his words. "So, they just dropped whatever they were doing, to come to help you?"

Nodding slowly, he said, "Yeah. Once a brother, always a brother."

She nodded, unsure what else to say. Seeing Chris

still standing over to the side, she asked, "How will I get back to Kansas?"

Eric nodded toward another small, private plane. "I've got a pilot to take us back there."

She blinked in surprise, and asked, "We're all going back? You're going back to Kansas, as well?"

He turned his body so they were facing each other, keeping his arms around her, enveloping her in his embrace. Holding her gaze, he said, "Lydia, I know we have a lot to talk about. First, and foremost, I want to get you back to your home in Kansas. We both need to debrief with the NBAF, and I know you've got friends and coworkers who want to see you, to be assured of your safety."

She nodded, understanding what he was saying but too afraid to ask him about their relationship. Before she had a chance to gather her courage, Chris called out, "The pilot says he's ready." Sucking in a deep breath, she let it out, and said, "Yesterday, the last thing I wanted to do was be back in another plane. But if this one is taking me home, I'll do it gladly."

Eric gave her another squeeze, then led her over to the plane. "I'll take you anywhere you want to go."

Two Days Later

Lydia awoke from her nightmare with a jolt, her

breathing ragged. Sitting up in bed, she looked around, recognizing her own bedroom, illuminated softly with a nightlight shining from the bathroom. Climbing from the bed, she padded into the bathroom and stared into the mirror. Dark circles were still underneath her eyes, and her complexion was pale. Splashing cold water on her face, she worked to steady her breathing.

Grabbing her robe from the hook on the back of the door, she wrapped herself in the thick chenille, tying it at her waist. No longer interested in sleep, she quietly walked out of her bedroom and into the kitchen.

"Can't sleep?"

She jumped, hating to show such fear in front of her daughter. Caroline moved forward, encircling her arms around her. They stood in the kitchen, hugging for a moment, she gaining strength from Caroline.

"I was sleeping," she said honestly. "I just think it's going to take me a while to not close my eyes and find myself back in…in…well, just back."

Caroline leaned away, and she stared into the face that was so similar to her own. Long dark hair. Chocolate eyes that were a little bit lighter than her own. They were almost the same height, but her daughter held the youthful appearance of someone on the blush of adulthood.

Letting her go, she fixed a pot of coffee and they sat down at the kitchen table. They chatted about college, Caroline's roommate, boys she had gone out with, her classes. She noticed that her daughter kept the conversation away from her own workplace, for which she was glad.

As the sun rose, sending the glow of sunshine through the kitchen window, she leaned back in her seat and let out a long breath. Holding Caroline's gaze, she said, "You know I appreciate you coming here, and you know I love you more than life itself. But you need to get back to college. Your life is there right now."

"Mom, you've always been there for me. Now, I want to be here for you."

She smiled and leaned forward, stretching her arm out to rest her hand on Caroline's. They linked fingers, the way they had ever since Caroline was very tiny and smiled at each other.

"I love having you here with me," she said. "But I've got some things that I need to get a handle on. I've got some decisions I need to make and, as much as I love having you with me, these are decisions that I'll have to make on my own."

"Are you going to work today?"

Nodding, she replied, "Yes. I'm going to go in, and we'll see what happens. Paul is supposed to meet with me, and I'm to have a debriefing on what all was happening and why. Eric explained a lot of things on the plane ride back from Portland, and I now know that Paul was involved in their mission…investigation… whatever it was."

"And Eric?"

Letting out a soft breath, she caught her gaze. "I don't really know what to say about him."

"Mom," Caroline said, giving her fingers a squeeze, "I saw you with him. I saw the way he was with you. That is not a man who was just doing his job. I have no

MARYANN JORDAN

doubt he would be right here with you, right now, if I wasn't here."

Shaking her head slightly, she said, "I told him I needed space—"

"Yes, and he's giving you that space because I'm here."

"Honey, I don't know what you want me to say. Yes, I really like him. I like him a lot. He's truly the only man that I've been with that I can say makes me think of the possibility of us lasting longer. But I have no idea what he does with his life or with his career. I have no idea how we could make something work, considering I now know that he's from Vermont. Right now, my mind is in such turmoil, the idea of trying to figure out anything is just too overwhelming."

She glanced down and noticed her coffee mug was now empty. Wanting to avoid Caroline's pointed stare, she stood and moved over to the sink to rinse out her cup.

She knew that she should be ecstatic right now. She was so lucky that everything had turned out okay. But... *Why do I feel as though I have a heavy blanket weighing me down?*

As though Caroline knew her thoughts, she said, "Mom, don't forget what the ER doctor recommended. You need to see a trauma counselor."

Afraid that the tears would renew, she simply nodded. Grateful her daughter understood, giving her a few minutes to pull herself together, she sucked in a deep breath before letting it out slowly. Turning, she enveloped Caroline in another hug. "I need to get ready to go in today. And you need to make arrangements to get back to school." Leaning back, she added, "Once I get things settled at work, I'm planning on taking some time off. If you think you can handle having your mom around, I'll come to visit you near Thanksgiving and stay for a little bit."

Caroline grinned widely. "I'd love that, Mom."

Forcing her arms to release her daughter, she touched Caroline's cheek before heading back to her bedroom. She had just enough time for a shower before going to work. Not having any idea what she was going to be facing today, she wondered if she was going to be seeing Eric, and her mind warred between the desire to be with him again and wondering when he was going to be leaving.

29

Eric met Lydia at the front of the building, unable to wait any longer to see her. As soon as they had arrived in Manhattan two days earlier, Caroline had whisked her away. Paul had contacted her to let her know what was going on, and Eric was grateful Lydia had her daughter there for her. His heart had been touched at the reunion between the two of them, both with tears streaming down their faces.

Still, he had not wanted to leave her alone. He wanted to be there for her, protect her, make sure she was okay. But Lydia was in a delicate state of mind and had needed her daughter with her. It had been difficult for him to back away, but he knew she needed some space. Unable to completely let go, he had insisted she see her family physician and was pleased when she had explained she had a trauma counselor recommendation she was going to follow up on. It was a start.

Now, as he watched her walking from the parking lot, he stepped directly up to her, wrapping his arms around her and kissing the top of her head.

He breathed easier when her arms encircled his waist, and she squeezed him back. He leaned away, just far enough to carefully look into her eyes, and asked, "Are you and Caroline doing okay?"

She nodded. "She's worried. On the one hand, I wish Paul hadn't called her and worried her so much. On the other hand," she shrugged and smiled slightly, "it's so nice to have her with me."

"Is she going to be able to stay for a while?"

Shaking her head, she replied, "I don't want her to do that. She has her studies. She has her life. I told her this morning that I want her to go ahead and make plans to get back."

Nodding, he watched as her gaze shifted beyond him to the NBAF building behind them. "Are you ready?"

"As ready as I'll ever be. I do want to see Beth and Jim, and I know Paul needs to talk to me." She shifted her gaze back to his, and asked, "Will you be there for that meeting?"

"I won't leave your side," he replied, leaning down to touch his lips to hers gently. He had spent the last two days thinking of nothing but her and how his life had changed since she came into it. He wanted to tell her that if she wanted, he would sell his place in Vermont and move to Kansas, but he held back, feeling that it was too soon, and she was too raw from her ordeal.

Sighing, he forced a smile on his face before linking fingers with her and escorting her inside the building.

He felt her stiffen as the guard did a double take when she walked by. Eric squeezed her fingers, and she sucked in a deep breath, squeezing his fingers in return. Most of the other employees passed on by, but her body remained stiff as they continued walking.

"Ignore them, Lydia," he whispered.

"I suddenly feel like a bug under the glass, but I suppose that's silly. I don't suppose anybody really knows."

"I know Paul kept it out of the news, and I doubt they wanted the word to get out around here."

Her feet stumbled just as they got to her lab area and he let go of her hand to wrap his arm around her shoulders. "Nobody but friends in here, Lydia."

She nodded, then sucked in a deep breath and pushed forward through the doors. She was immediately engulfed by Beth, who practically threw herself at her, and he placed his hands on her waist to steady her. Jim joined the group hug and Eric stepped back, giving them a chance to greet her.

He had come to the NBAF the previous day to fill Jim and Beth in on everything that he could tell them so they would not ply her with questions today. He looked on gratefully as they stepped back after their hug, simply saying if she needed anything, to let them know. They moved back to their workstations, and she turned around to look at him.

"When do we need to meet with Paul?"

He linked fingers with her again and pulled her closer. "Let's go ahead and get this over with." Paul had told him that whenever Lydia was ready, to come

273

MARYANN JORDAN

to his office, but he did not want to put it off any longer.

She blew out another breath and nodded, and they walked down the hall toward the administrative offices. Paul's assistant looked up as they walked in and offered a quick smile before immediately showing them into Paul's office.

He felt Lydia's entire body quiver, and he shot Paul a pointed look over her head, hoping to indicate that they needed to keep this quick and simple. He breathed easier when Paul gave him a nearly imperceptible nod before moving over and enveloping Lydia in a hug.

"Thank God you're all right," Paul said. He pulled back and held her by the shoulders, staring into her face. "Come and sit down, Lydia. I'm just going to give you the basic information that you need to know, understanding of course, that you have already given your official statement to the DHS."

Eric held a chair out for her to sit and then shifted his chair close to her's, putting his arm around her shoulder once again.

Paul moved to a chair near her as well and settled. Holding her gaze, he began. "DHS became aware of North Korea's interest in developing diseases that could be spread amongst farm animals. Meat is a staple of many diets around the world, so you can imagine the ramifications if they were successful, especially in poor areas. Of course, they also wanted to know how to protect themselves while developing and nurturing these diseases. Even though they have doctors, scien-

274

tists, and researchers, they lag far behind the work that we do here."

He paused, as though to give Lydia a chance to absorb this information, and Eric looked to the side, seeing her offer a simple nod. He looked back at Paul and waited for him to continue.

"Since we opened this facility, we've had our eye on the local groups and the extremists, as well. As you know, their goal is to disrupt the research that we have here. Some information came our way recently that connected the two events. Basically, there have been suspicions of money coming in from North Korea to one of the extremist groups. On top of this, the seminar on African Swine Fever was already in place, with international journalists and researchers coming to see our facility. We recognized this was a prime opportunity for North Korea to make a move. Send someone in, gather as much information as possible and, if needed, the extremist group was here to back them up."

Paul glanced toward him, and he nodded. When he talked to Paul yesterday, he informed him that he wanted Lydia to be aware of the entire scope of the mission, including his part.

Focusing on Lydia again, Paul said, "Eric was hired by someone at DHS to come here and pose as a journalist. His mission was to keep an eye on the other journalists, assess their behavior, ferret out any possible double dealers, that sort of thing. We also had assigned some of our DHS to be with the scientists who were in other parts of the facility here."

"Ji-Ho…was he the only one who was an imposter?" Lydia asked.

"Yes," Paul replied. "Eric had discovered that the money trail led back to a man named Hyun-Gi, but it wasn't until we arressted him that night, and you corrobarated his identity, that we discovered he and Ji-Ho were the same man. The scientists were all who they said they were, and so were the other journalists. He was the only one who came in with a fake South Korean passport and identity."

"I still don't understand what he was trying to do here," she confessed, her gaze moving between he and Paul.

"That's where I come in, I believe."

He and Lydia swung their heads around and watched as Linda Hughley walked into the room. Lydia quickly stood as Linda approached.

"Lydia, I'm so sorry that there was confusion between us," Linda said. She offered a hug to Lydia, before they both sat down.

Paul continued, "It appears that Hyun-Gi had multiple agendas here. For one, he wanted to gather intel on our security systems. For another, he wanted to get as much info on our research and procedures as he could. In the end, he decided their best course of action was to take Linda back with them. Which is where Robert came in. He had been paying Robert for some time and blackmailed him into kidnapping what was supposed to be the head of the African Swine Fever division, obviously Linda. Robert mixed up Linda

Hughley with Lydia Hughes and made his fatal error in kidnapping the wrong person."

"Unbelievable…it's all so unbelievable," Lydia said, shaking her head. "He told me that he had a way to get out of the country. That was what he was going to do with Linda. He was going to get her back to North Korea."

Her voice had risen with each word, and Eric wrapped his arm around her again, pulling her close. He hoped his body was giving her strength and noticed her breathing evened.

Paul nodded. "He's now in custody. What will happen to him remains to be seen, but, yes, he and his compatriots had planned on taking her back to North Korea. As far as we can tell, they had planned on taking a small boat out of the harbor in Washington state and then transfering Linda to another ship, probably keeping her drugged the whole time."

Not wanting Lydia to relive her ordeal needlessly, since she had already given her report to DHS already, Paul and Linda stood and offered her hugs once more. Linda left the room, and Paul moved to stand directly in front of Lydia.

"I want you to take as much time off as you need. I know you've been given a list of trauma counselors, and we want to make sure that you start seeing them. I cannot begin to imagine the horror that you went through, but we at DHS and here at this facility, support you in whatever you need to do."

Eric watched her carefully, glad when he did not see

renewed tears. Instead, she smiled slightly and nodded. "Thank you, Paul. I...well...I have no idea right now what I want to do or need to do. I don't want to just sit at home and do nothing, but I'm not ready to come back and work here right now. Caroline is going back east, and I thought I might join her for a little extended vacation."

Paul smiled warmly. "I think that's an excellent idea, Lydia. Take as much time as you need."

Eric led Lydia back outside the NBAF, and when they reached her car, she stopped and turned, looking back at the building. He did not want to disturb her train of thought, so he remained silent for a few minutes. She slowly seemed to become aware of her surroundings again and looked at him, blushing.

"I'm sorry...lost in thought, I suppose."

He stepped closer and reached his hands up to cup her face. "Don't ever apologize for taking time to figure out what you need." He leaned forward and, once again, placed a sweet kiss on her lips.

She stared into his face and whispered, "Will I ever see you again, after you leave here?"

He continued to cup her face and smiled. "I wanted to wait and tell you this when you were stronger, because I want you to focus on you right now. But, Lydia, I want to be with you. You're in my heart and that's where I want you to stay."

She offered a tremulous smile, and said, "I care so much for you. I want to be with you also, but I need to get my life back on track. I was honest with Paul, telling him that I wanted to head back east and visit my parents and spend a little time near Caroline. She's actually already looked up a trauma counselor near her college campus."

He sucked in a deep breath before letting it out slowly. "I think that's a good idea. Selfishly, I'm glad that we'll be on the same side of the country for a little while. But I know you have a lot to think about. I'll give you all my contact information. I hope that you'll use it when you're ready."

Unheeding of the others in the parking lot, he held her face, his thumbs sweeping her cheeks. Bending, he kissed her again, this time with all the emotion he felt churning inside. Love and hope, desire and need. He felt her hands tighten on his waist and the burn of each fingertip was like a brand. One he did not want to extinguish.

Their tongues tangled as he memorized the taste, touch, and essence of her. Finally, leaning back a slight inch, he drew in a ragged breath. His heart ached, and as much as he hated seeing her cry, this time her tears were for him and that sent a sliver of comfort through him, knowing she was as affected as he was.

"I don't know how to let you go," she confessed, swallowing deeply, blinking as another tear slid down her cheek.

"Then, let's not say goodbye," he said, holding her gaze. "I know we've said we weren't making promises, but I love you, Lydia. You take all the time you need. I'll wait for you."

Her breath caught in her throat, and she hiccupped a sob. "I love you, too."

With a final kiss goodbye, he watched her drive

away, his eyes never leaving her car until it was out of sight. He rubbed his chest, feeling heartache deep inside. She made him want things in life that he thought were over…a woman to love and cherish. One to wake up to each morning. One to laugh with, share with, grow old with. Closing his eyes for a moment, he wondered if he would ever see her again. He knew that once they were no longer together, her feelings could change. Sucking in a deep breath, he headed to his car.

He drove to the car rental store, dropped off his vehicle, and was picked up by Chris, who drove them back to the Kansas City airport. Chris was unusually quiet on the drive so, when they finally arrived, he asked, "Are you okay?"

Nodding, Chris replied, "I thought I was ready for fieldwork but everything that happened with Lydia… well, let's just say that maybe I'm better off doing my computer work in an office."

"Chris, I wouldn't have found Lydia if it hadn't been for you. If I had not had someone with your talent and skill along with us, this mission would never have been successful."

Chris grinned, blush rising over his face, and he laughed. "Just make sure you're doing what you want to do. You want to work in an office, that's great. But if you ever want to do fieldwork again, I'm letting Silas know that you're the man to have."

He stuck out his hand for a shake, but Chris grabbed him and pulled him in for a hug. Saying goodbye, he bent and grabbed his bag and walked into the airport.

As the plane left the ground, he looked down and

saw the vast Kansas vista spread out before him. Rolling hills. Large ranches. Green and tan prairies. As he contemplated the possibility of moving there, he realized that would be okay. If Lydia would have him, he would move anywhere to be with her.

Now, he just had to wait to see if she would have him.

30

The sun had risen over Caspian Lake, the lights sparkling across the surface. Eric's feet pounded a staccato as he ran along the path leading from the deep woods toward his house. His mind was a jumble of thoughts, remembering his visitor right after he returned from Kansas. Silas Branson had appeared on his porch, much like he had the previous time, now offering his congratulations for a mission well accomplished.

As they had shared a cup of coffee, sitting on his porch overlooking the lake, he had been reminded of how many changes had occurred since the first time they had done so. When Silas had asked him if he would be available for other missions, he had had to think for several, long moments.

"Silas, I'm not exactly sure how to answer that. I suppose if nothing much changes in my life, then I would agree to take another mission for you. But..."

Silas' lips curved into a smile, and he said, "I assume the *but*, is whether or not you and Lydia Hughes decide to…well, decide to do something. Right?"

He nodded slowly, thinking how much he missed Lydia, but also knowing that he had not heard from her in weeks. "You're right. I don't know if that's going to happen, but I can still hope."

"And, if you could lead a team from here? Not go into the field, but plan and coordinate?"

He swung his head around, giving Silas a pointed stare. "Like Logan?"

Nodding, Silas said, "Yeah, very much like him."

His lips curved slightly as he gave it some thought, and he said, "That I could do."

They stood and shook hands. Clapping him on the back, Silas walked back to his dark SUV and pulled out of Eric's drive.

That was almost three weeks ago, and he had had no more visitors since then. As he continued jogging up the path, he saw a figure on his back porch again. He slowed his pace, his heart stuttering as he viewed who was there. Stopping, with his hands on his hips, he grinned upward. "You're a sight for sore eyes, Lydia Hughes."

She leaned over, resting her palms on the wooden railing of the deck and smiled down at him. "Took me a while to find this place. You're really off the beaten path." She lifted her gaze and cast it toward the lake behind him. "But, it's worth the search. The view is breathtaking."

"Yeah, it is," he agreed, his eyes never leaving her. He

jogged around to the deck stairs, taking them two at a time. When he reached the top, his feet did not stop until he was directly in front of her. "I missed you." He realized how inadequate the words sounded, but they were the only thing he could think of.

He stepped closer, taking her hands in his, not wanting any space between them. His chest hurt just seeing her, but his heart leaped as soon as his fingers wrapped around hers. "How are you?" he asked.

"Better," she said, a smile on her face. "I'm better."

"Have you been with Caroline?"

Her smile widened, and she nodded. "Yes. We spent Thanksgiving with my parents, and then I stayed at a little bed and breakfast near her campus."

"I'm glad. I know it's been good for you to take time for yourself."

"It was, but she's an adult now and hardly needs her mother hanging around. It was nice to meet her friends and see her dorm. It's been lovely to go out to eat occasionally with her, but she has her own life."

He hesitated, and then asked, "Did you speak to a trauma counselor?"

A shadow passed through her eyes for just a fleeting few seconds, but she sucked in a deep breath and nodded. "Yes, I've gone twice weekly for the past two weeks. A lot of what I've needed was just to talk about the events in a safe environment without someone who was emotionally involved. I still wake up a little shaken some nights, but it's getting better. I no longer look over my shoulder constantly. Of course, I'll keep it up as needed."

He reached up and tucked a wind-blown strand of hair behind her ear. "I'm glad."

She held his gaze. "I've also been processing several things in my life."

Uncertain of her meaning, he tilted his head to the side slightly. "What kind of things?" he asked, his gut clenching at the possible meaning of her words.

"My life has been a little harder to figure out. I told you that I took the job at NBAF because of the stability, benefits, and it allowed Caroline to finish out at the high school there in Manhattan where she had started. It was a good place to work, but it was never my dream job." She held his gaze and added, "That's still true."

"And your dream job is...?" he prodded, linking his fingers with hers tighter.

She sucked in a deep breath of fresh air and let it out slowly, and he noticed the color in her cheeks was vibrant and her eyes sparkled.

"I want to go back to working as a country vet. That was always my goal. Work alongside farmers with their cattle, goats, pigs. I can even do small animals like rabbits, cats, and dogs. I want to get to know my neighbors and their pets. I want to get to know the local farmers and know that I'm helping them with their stock. I'm glad that there are researchers, but that environment was never my career goal."

He smiled. "I can tell you're giving me the truthful answer, because your face is glowing." He started to ask her another question, but she beat him to it.

"What about you? Now that you've had a taste for missions again, is that your new pursuit?"

Shaking his head slowly, he said, "No, not really. After this last mission, I've come to understand that I appreciate the peace and quiet. I told them that I would not mind helping plan and coordinate, but that I don't want to be sent out into the field again."

They stood, side by side, quietly for a moment, looking out over the thick forest leading down to the crystal blue lake. His heart pounded with nerves as he slid his eyes sideways, and asked, "For your dream job, where do you want to be?"

He watched as she turned her head slowly toward him, her eyes seeking his. Drawing in another deep breath, as though to settle her nerves, she replied, "I don't really care where my job is, as long as I can be near you. That is, if you still want me."

He threw his head back, the sun warm on his face, and whooped loudly, before grabbing her around the waist, lifting her, and twirling around in circles. "From the first night we spent together, I felt something for you," he said. "And then the first time I saw you sitting on your ass surrounded by pigs, I knew I wanted to be with you." She laughed along with him, holding onto his shoulders as he slowly lowered her back to the deck.

With her still in his arms, he bent down, taking her lips in a kiss. Her firm body pressed tightly against his. The tangle of her thick hair against his fingers. Her lips, warm and pliant, underneath his. He wanted to memorize every second of the kiss, hardly believing that they would be sharing a lifetime of them. The kiss represented everything he felt for her, sealing them together.

One Year Later

Eric drove along the Vermont country road, the lush green pastures extending on either side of him. Turning onto another lane that ran along a fenced pasture, he observed the cattle in the fields. As he neared the house with the barn in the back, he pulled around to where he could see the farmer talking with Lydia.

She was wearing faded jeans, a long-sleeved t-shirt, covered by a thick jacket, and her feet were encased in knee-high rubber boots covered in mud, muck, and God knows what else. Her hair was pulled back in a pony-tail, although a few tendrils blew in the breeze.

Unable to keep the grin from his face, he watched as she talked excitedly, her hands waving around, obviously into her story. The farmer's head reared back as he roared with laughter and Eric laughed as well, even though he had no idea what they were talking about. He loved seeing the bright smile and energy radiating from her.

Climbing down from his truck, he walked over. Shaking Mr. Maguildy's hand, he greeted Lydia with a hug.

"I'm so sorry you had to come," she began.

He shushed her. "You do know this is it for your old car? I'm buying you a new one tomorrow."

"But—"

"No buts," he retorted with a pretend glare, but he knew she could see the twinkle in his eyes.

"Listen to your husband," Mr. Maguildy said. "I'll get my son to work on your junker here, and we'll get it back to you, but I agree with Eric. A farm vet needs a good, reliable vehicle."

She nodded, and as they walked to his truck, she looked back longingly toward her old car. "That thing brought me here all the way from Kansas."

"Yep," he agreed. "And now it's time to put it out to pasture."

She barked out a laugh as they climbed into his truck. "Oh, bad pun," she giggled, reaching out to clasp his hand in hers, giving it a squeeze.

Thirty minutes later, they parked outside their house on Caspian Lake. Inside, she immediately headed to the shower, and he grabbed the steaks out of the refrigerator where they were marinating. Stepping onto the deck, he fired up the grill.

She soon joined him and encircled her arms around his waist from behind, pressing her cheek between his shoulder blades.

Once the steaks were sizzling, he twisted around and encircled her with his arms as well. "Thought we'd have the steaks Paul sent," he murmured, his mouth pressed against the top of her head.

"Mmmm, a taste of Kansas all the way here in Vermont."

"You sorry?" he asked.

She leaned back and looked up quizzically. "Sorry?"

"About moving from Kansas?"

She smiled, and said, "Not as long as I've got friends who can send me beef." Her smile drooped slightly, and she lifted a hand to cup his cheek, staring into his eyes. "You know the answer to that, Eric. Out there, I had a life but wasn't really living. Now, with Caroline happily in school and me here with you...this is all I want."

He moved the barest inch needed to place a kiss on her lips, reveling in the feel and touch of her skin. "I had a life here also, but until you, I wasn't living either," he admitted.

"How long will it take the steaks to cook?" she asked, her lips still pressed against his.

"Not long," he said, then grinned widely. "But, if you're in the mood for a quickie, we should be able to take care of that."

Laughing, she ran into the house with him quickly on her heels.

31

SEVEN YEARS LATER

Eric sat in the rocking chair, the early dawn just beginning to peek through the windows. He had given up his early morning run for a much better activity, staring down at one-month-old Lisa. Her tiny face wiggled ever so slightly as she continued to sleep. He knew the house would soon be awake and alive with energy and cherished his few moments of quiet time with her.

Hearing a noise at the door, he looked up and smiled. Lydia, wrapped in a bright red robe tied at the waist, leaned her shoulder against the doorframe.

"I see you've claimed Lisa early this morning," she said, her smile warm upon him.

Keeping his voice soft, he replied, "I figured I'd better enjoy her while I can, before the Christmas chaos begins."

She nodded her understanding and pushed off from the doorframe, taking only a few steps into the room when a small boy rushed past her, calling, "Mom! Dad! Come on—Santa's been here!"

Before he had a chance to respond to his son, Caroline hurried in. "Oh, my goodness, thank you Eric. I can't believe I didn't hear her, but the extra half hour of sleep for Bill and me was wonderful!" She bent and took her daughter from his arms, and said, "Let me nurse her, and then we'll be downstairs."

He kissed his granddaughter's head before leaning over and kissing Caroline's cheek. Looking down at Eric Jr., he said, "Let's go, bud. Let's find out what Santa brought you."

Wrapping his arm around Lydia's shoulders as they followed their exuberant six-year-old son downstairs, he knew he was living the dream that, at one time, he had thought had passed him by. He had a wife he loved and adored, and she had given him a child, when he never thought fatherhood was possible.

And, in marrying Lydia, he gained an adult daughter in Caroline, who welcomed him with open arms. He had thought his heart would burst with pride as he walked Caroline down the aisle. And now, having a granddaughter to love, brought his world full-circle.

Settling onto the sofa, he viewed the decorated Christmas tree next to the stone fireplace, and Caspian Lake in the distance through the windows. His son's shouts of glee as he tore open his presents brought a smile to his face. Caroline and her husband, Bill, sat on the loveseat with Lisa nestled in Caroline's arms. He looked up to see Lydia walking into the room, a tray of homemade cinnamon rolls and coffee cups in her hand.

As soon as she set the tray on the coffee table, he reached over and snagged her hand, gently pulling her onto his lap. She wrapped her arms around his neck and kissed him softly on the lips.

"Merry Christmas, baby," he said, his arms tight around her.

"Merry Christmas," she replied. "Happy?"

Casting his gaze once more about the room before staring back at her, he said, "There's nothing more Santa could bring me that would make me happier than I am right now with my family here together." He watched as her eyes misted, and he grinned. Placing a light kiss on her lips, they were interrupted by their son's excited shout.

That evening, as the sun set over lake, he watched the evening shadows deepen. Sitting on his deck, facing the water, he propped his feet on the rail as the moon began to rise. Wrapped warmly against the Vermont December weather, he sipped his scotch whiskey.

He appreciated the view and the whiskey, but as he heard his family laughing inside, he did not miss the quiet that he had grown accustomed to. As he sipped the last of his drink, he placed his hands on the arms of his chair and hoisted his body upward. As usual, his knee twinged, reminding him of days gone by.

Moving through the sliding glass door and setting the alarm, he turned with a wide smile on his face. Everything he ever wanted was right there in that room. All of his loved ones, together.

Don't miss any news about new releases! Sign up for my
Newsletter

If you liked SEAL Together, check out the other books
by me!
Maryann Jordan

Lighthouse Security Investigations
Mace
Rank

Baytown Boys (small town, military romantic suspense)
Coming Home
Just One More Chance
Clues of the Heart
Finding Peace
Picking Up the Pieces
Sunset Flames
Waiting for Sunrise
Hear My Heart

Follow the exciting spin-off series:
Alvarez Security (military romantic suspense)
Gabe
Tony
Vinny
Jobe

Saints Protection & Investigations
(an elite group, assigned to the cases no one else
wants…or can solve)

Serial Love
Healing Love
Seeing Love
Honor Love
Sacrifice Love
Remember Love
Discover Love
Surviving Love
Celebrating Love

Letters From Home (military romance)
Class of Love
Freedom of Love
Bond of Love

The Love's Series (detectives)
Love's Taming
Love's Tempting
Love's Trusting

The Fairfield Series (small town detectives)
Emma's Home
Laurie's Time
Carol's Image
Fireworks Over Fairfield

Please take the time to leave a review of this book. Feel free to contact me, especially if you enjoyed my book. I love to hear from readers!
Facebook
Email

Website

Made in the USA
Coppell, TX
25 September 2023

22016432R00177